Beers Abroad

Also by P.M. LaRose

Beers Ahead
Bet on Beers
First Case of Beers

Beers Abroad

Peril in London

P.M. LaRose

liquid
rabbit
publishing

Cover design and illustration by P.M. LaRose

Liquid Rabbit Publishing
2010 Glasgow Ave.
Baton Rouge, LA 70808

pmlarose.com
email: BeersAhead@gmail.com
Facebook: PM LaRose
Facebook: Beers Detective Agency

ISBN 978-1-7324951-3-5

First Edition: October 2019
10 9 8 7 6 5 4 3 2 1

For Rosa, whose smile
and humor inspired me

You don't pull the mask off that old lone ranger
And you don't mess around with Jim

—"You Don't Mess Around With Jim," Jim Croce

Prologue

The body count during my London vacation was three. By that point, I had decided the world of commerce was not my cup of tea.

I had no idea what was to come, nor did I want to find out.

A mugging, several murders, a bombing—and I thought Britain was more civilized than the Wild West.

This is definitely not what I signed up for.

IN CASE you're wondering what I *did* sign up for, it was to be head of security for a department store in Minneapolis, Minnesota, US of A. Not across the ocean, dodging a killer—or maybe two?—while piecing together the clues of yet another mystery in which I had become unwittingly involved.

But let's just back up a little so you get the whole picture.

The name's Jim. James A. Biersovich for the record, Beers for short. Back in the good old days, I used to be a sportswriter. Well, they weren't such good old days. That's why I quit when I hit 40 and took a chance on this department store gig.

Call it an existential crisis or just acting on a whim. It got me out of the going-nowhere rut of fashioning third-grade-level prose about inconsequential sporting matters in an effort to earn myself some jack while entertaining the public.

Because let's just tell it like it is. Sports is entertainment, nothing more. It doesn't solve world hunger or negotiate peace or battle crime. It's just a medium to amuse the masses. And for the life of me, I couldn't understand how on God's gray earth my writing about junior high field hockey matches could be in the least bit entertaining.

I've always tried to be logical like that. Maybe I over-analyze.

Anyway, when a suit at the department store offered me an exit lane, I took it. Little did I realize I would on a regular basis come face to face with life-or-death situations—with the latter occurring far too often.

Here I was just past my second anniversary at La Scala, the tony department store in downtown Minnehooha, and once again I was terrified. Terror seemed to be the uniform for the job. It fit me like a straitjacket.

Ostensibly, my role at the store was to handle the routine tasks of securing modern merchandising—averting shoplifting, maintaining door locks, escorting the fire marshals on their annual inspection tours and other mundane considerations. No one told me murder played such an integral role in commerce.

So, as I have done in previous reports, I should start from the beginning. Otherwise, it will be hard to put the current dilemma in context.

Following the gruesome events of Halloween (see previous case history for details), the Christmas holidays were relatively uneventful. Except that I made great headway in my relationship with my current flame.

Like I said, I work in a department store and so does my girlfriend, Emmie Slayton. She was the best thing that happened during the gory Halloween episode. I could describe her beauty, her charm, her wit, but some things I'd rather keep personal.

Emmie and I spent lots of quality time getting to know each other better over Christmas, and even survived dinner with Dad and his girlfriend, Jane Mertin—my former boss, Emmie's current boss. Talk about convoluted relationships. Jane brought her younger son, Lex, a 20-year-old slacker who repeatedly called me "bro," to my disdain.

Emmie gave me a rare Beatles album, *Yesterday and Today* with the butcher cover. I'm certain she had help coming up with the idea since she was born practically day before yesterday ("So Very Young" pops into mind), but I wasn't asking questions. It was a great present. My gift to her was more practical. Everyone needs luggage on wheels, right?

In the middle of Minnesnowta's annual deluge of white precipitation, my buddy Freddie managed to drag me out to a course and introduce me to snow golf. I didn't see that it would stick as a preferred pastime because I spent more time hunting for the ball than actual golfing. By the way, Freddie is my drinking buddy, the lone remaining friend from my days at the Minnesota Herald. Freddie's got issues, and I don't mean the daily edition kind.

There were down sides to the season, naturally. On one particularly icy morning, a coed came skidding out of an alley into the path of my 1972 Dodge Dart, a classic I had nurtured since my college days, and put a nasty dent in the front right fender. Dings, dents, crunches are a way of life in that godforsaken frozen tundra. They're unavoidable. Cars are not ice skates.

When the street glaciers receded after another excruciating season of cold, gaping chasms were left in their wake, lurking to swallow unsuspecting vehicles. The Dart met its demise at the clutches of one of these car-killers, a hole disguised as a shallow puddle that turned out to be cavernous and succeeded in destroying an axle.

Every year, winter ice tears up the streets. Every spring, Band-aids are applied to the holes. They might as well put toothpaste or chunky peanut butter in the potholes for all the good that does. I don't understand why they don't put down something more permanent, like what they use to make black boxes for airplanes. But I guess that's job security for the road patchers.

At that point, the Dart was a goner, and I thought it best to acquire wheels of a more recent vintage. I briefly considered buying a moped instead of a car, but the prospect of getting even chummier with winter quashed that idea. The 2000 program car I settled on, a Corolla, isn't very sexy, but it seems dependable. At least this one has a CD player built in, and I don't have to open the glove compartment to load music into a tape deck.

Which brings us more or less up to date.

Like I said, my name's Jim and I'm 40 and change. With alarmingly thinning hair and equally disturbing thickening gut, I am your prototypical humanoid trying to survive in a hostile world.

That it is hostile I have no doubt. And much of the hostility is man-made, as you'll see from my report.

1

Friday, April 6, 2001
Dateline: London

So here we are in the landmark year of 2001. A famous year. They made a movie about it, which I've seen several times. I'm not quite sure what it means—maybe only Stanley Kubrick, the director, understood it.

It is April and I've arrived in London, my first visit to the U.K. Lena and I have, I mean. Lena appears to handle adversity better than I do. She just seems to roll with the punches, whereas I'm usually knocked down for the count. Knocked out literally, a couple of times.

By the way, Lena is Lena Fangeaux. She works in the jewelry department on the fifth floor back at La Scala of Minneapolis, when she's not assisting me.

I guess I'd better fill in a few more blanks here. Unlike my reporting days, when inverted pyramid was the style du jour, this story needs to start at the beginning.

Johnny Scalabrino, the big cheese in the La Scala constellation, sent us to London to follow up on his earlier scouting trip. He was looking for a location for store number five in his growing empire. He got it into his head that he could compete with the old guard of London's retail industry—Harrods, Harvey Nichols, Fenwick, Selfridges.

Scalabrino envisioned setting up shop alongside Hyde Park in the heart of the shopping district and offering his Italian style to the neighborhood. Each store in the La Scala chain has a theme. At the original location, where I work, it's the classic architecture of Italy. The Colosseum, the canals of Venice, the Vatican, the Appian

13

Way and other landmarks are depicted in wall-size murals across its floors.

In Las Vegas, it's a Hollywood theme, with various artifacts of Italian celebrities, Scalabrino's private collection, scattered around the store. Chicago takes a grittier tone, with Al Capone, Lucky Luciano, Joe Valachi, Joseph Bonanno and other gangsters shown in scenes from their reigns of terror.

San Francisco's design is based on the wines of Italy, playing off the California wine country. Not sure what he plans to make the overriding motif of the London outlet, but I'm certain he'll find some Italian angle.

I visited the Chicago store shortly after Scalabrino put me in charge of security for the whole chain. This was the result of my cracking the head-in-a-box case. I didn't think I'd like working in Chicago, because all those mobsters wielding gats staring down at me every day would freak me out.

Anyway, Lena and I arrived here in London with the charge of looking at a couple of prime locations for Scalabrino's foray into international commerce. One is a failed apartment complex, which seemed like a stretch due to the construction involved. The other is an abandoned warehouse which has gone through any number of incarnations over the years.

I know all this because Lena, dispatched as my assistant, is ace at electronic research. After a couple of visits to London's property bureaus and libraries, she was able to assemble fairly complete histories of the structures going back a couple of centuries.

Actually, I should say locations because the current structures are considerably less than centuries old. They're also far short of being habitable, due to the bombing at the warehouse and problems too numerous to list at the apartment building.

So, let's see. Where to begin...pardon me while I scan my notes. I have to do that, otherwise I wouldn't remember anything. The reporter's notepad that I still carry everywhere is my portable computer. It knows far more than I do, or can recall.

There aren't too many artifacts remaining from my reporting career—well, there's Freddie—but the notepad is vital. I'm constantly taking notes, which is why I can reproduce all these conversations verbatim.

Like I say, it began with Scalabrino's desire to open a London outlet. After a couple of preliminary exploratory trips, where I understand he spent more time at the London Playboy Club than actual looking for a store location, he sent Lena and me to further investigate the final two candidates.

He assured me this would be a crime-free mission, simply scoping out the sites and looking into what it would take in time and money to get a building ready for occupation. We were asked to examine each site for habitability, design, security requirements, already installed facilities such as sprinkler systems and alarms, egress points, including integrity of the doors, and any hidden defects we might find.

In addition, we would need to research the crime rate in the area and accessibility to security services and locksmiths, parking availability, proximity to public transport, plus have the boiler and air conditioning inspected. The electronic research I would leave to Lena, who was the expert in that field.

In my spare time, Scalabrino said, I might steal ideas from other merchants such as Harrods. Steal. Nice terminology for a store owner to use.

Our first stop in London after dropping our gear at the hotel was the office of Charlene McAllen, the estate agent Scalabrino had lined up to show us the properties. She was a nice-looking woman about my age, maybe a few years older, with deep brown hair curled at the ends and wearing a sharp and well-fitted gray pantsuit. I could sense Lena sizing her up, as women are known to do in such situations.

"Jim Biersovich," I said, shaking her hand.

"Very pleased to meet you," Charlene said. "And you must be Lena...Fan-geeks is it?"

"Fan-GO, like da awtist, Vincent," Lena replied. "Although some of my family from Labadieville say it like Fawn-JOO. Dey jus' puttin' on airs."

Charlene presented us with a pair of packets on the sites in question, giving dimensions, floor plans, current taxes, estimated value across the last couple of decades and building codes for that zone. In addition, since both were in a designated historic district, they had further restrictions dictated by the landmark commission.

"Well, shall we begin?" Charlene asked, pushing back from her desk and rising. "My car's round back."

"Shotgun!" Lena yelled.

Charlene led us through the back entrance to a kelly green Land Rover adjacent to the building. Lena ran ahead and opened the front passenger door, only to find herself behind the wheel. She got a little red in the face as she exited and went around to the other side. Charlene was smirking, but I was laughing outright.

"Shut up, Beers," she said as we headed off to our first destination. I would have pointed out that the Brits do things a bit differently, but I didn't want to push Lena too far. I needed her on my side.

The apartment building was kitty-corner from Harrods, the most famous of London's classic department stores. Street level housed a comics emporium on one side, a shuttered camera shop on the other. The rest of the seven floors were vacant of tenants.

Charlene unlocked an unmarked door between the shops and led us up a steep flight of stairs to the second floor, the initial level of flats. Hallways headed off in both directions, then around corners. She opened the door of the nearest street-side unit, which was unlocked, and we walked through. The most attractive aspect of the space was a picture window overlooking Brompton Road, with a view of Harrods' entrance. Patrons flowed in and out of the store at a brisk clip. Scalabrino would have his work cut out for him in trying to lure clientele from that establishment.

Across the hall were apartments with decidedly less appeal—no windows. It appeared the building was more intended for office space than living quarters. I couldn't imagine inhabiting an apartment that had no outside view. It would feel like a tomb, which is the impression I got from this dirty and dingy structure.

It also felt closed in because there was no air circulating. Lena wrinkled her nose at every room we entered. Even I had to hold my breath occasionally due to a particularly strong musty or acrid odor.

Charlene apologized for the state of the building. "It's been closed up for nigh on a year. The owner realized he made a mistake early on when he couldn't maintain half occupancy. All he saw was proximity to Harrods, and pound notes danced in his head. As you can gather, it's not the ideal design for flats."

"Smells like sumpin' died in heah," Lena muttered as we walked the floor.

No sooner had Lena uttered these words than we came upon the source of the stench, a mound of blankets in the corner of one of the rooms. It stopped us cold. I immediately imagined the worst—someone had been murdered. And by the aroma, quite some time ago.

A soft snore emanated from the foul-smelling heap, indicating the presence of a human in repose, much to our relief. We quickly backed out and Charlene apologized.

"Gentlemen of the streets are quick to find their way into any abandoned site," she explained. "It's a problem. London has available services, but some people prefer their independence."

Up the stairs we went, stopping only briefly on each floor. There were few distinguishing features until we got to the top level. Half the interior units were taken over by what used to be a workout space, now just an abandoned atrium where the sun beamed down on a torn exercise mat that covered a segment of the speckled linoleum floor. In the corner was a punctured medicine ball spilling its sandy guts. A chinning bar in a doorway was bent down in the middle. The door led to a shower room, whose creeping mold content caused us to make a hasty retreat.

Charlene offered to show us the basement, where the boiler room and elevator car could be inspected, but I declined. Lena concurred. "Dis place is a dump, heah. Scalabrino ain't got enough bread ta make it into a stoah."

"It is a bit rough," Charlene admitted. "Initial outlay for retrofitting would be substantial, granted, but the property can be had for a song."

What song? I wondered. The only thing appropriate that came to mind was "Demolition" by the Kinks. That would be my recommendation, anyway.

2

A few notes about Lena. For one, she's brilliant. I'm not sure what her degree is in, but she's a technical guru, to me.

You probably wouldn't realize how bright she is for two reasons. One, she looks like a Victoria's Secret model—tall, blond, very well proportioned, angelic face. Someone that good-looking couldn't be smart also, right?

The second reason is when she talks, her accent makes her sound less intelligent than she really is. That's the hazard of being a yat. The unique patois of New Orleans residents unfairly marks them as lower class, lacking in refinement.

But Lena is the picture of elegance, always looks snazzy and, despite the accent, is way more cultured than you would suspect. How she has remained single into her mid-30s is amazing, but I suppose she has pretty high standards, and most of the guys I know wouldn't measure up. I know I wouldn't.

Although I consider myself an average male specimen—not too tall, not too fat or thin, not too dense—I hadn't had a great track record with the ladies until Emmie came along. When I looked in the mirror, I saw Charlton Heston stepping in to save the day. One of my detractors, our muscle-bound but effeminate window dresser, once called me the spitting image of Charlie McCarthy. But I'm no dummy.

Following the events of the trick-or-treating season, my job became more important. Scalabrino decided to make me an offer I couldn't refuse. No, not like that. He promoted me.

Formerly a lowly aide to a vice president, I was named security chief for the entire La Scala chain. Not quite VP level, but higher than the peon I was previously.

My elevated employment status meant I finally got moved out of my minuscule broom closet of an office on the ninth floor into a more spacious broom closet down the hall. It's so spacious, in fact, Lena has a small desk across from me and there are *two* chairs for visitors. Of course, Lena isn't always there. I couldn't quite shake her loose from the jewelry counter full time. She is reluctant to give up the commissions, seeing as she is one of the top saleswomen.

The main drawback is it's farther down the hall from my beautiful Emmie, but I guess I can use the exercise. At least it has a window, so I can check the weather every now and then to see how much snow is piling up.

HAVING SEEN all we could stomach of this abandoned apartment building and immediately writing it off in my mind, we headed back down and out to the sidewalk. Lena decided she wanted to explore, and I had an idea exactly where as she crossed toward Harrods.

Charlene and I popped into the comics shop, where she left her card and asked the clerk to have the owner ring her.

Back in her car, we set out for her office.

"Your girlfriend is lovely," she said, as we waited at a light.

"No, no, she's not my girlfriend. She's a co-worker."

"Still. Wonderful accent."

"She's from New Orleans."

"Well, that explains it now, doesn't it?"

"Lena is my assistant. I'm the director of security for the La Scala department store chain."

"I see. And you're here to...?"

I wasn't sure how much Scalabrino had explained or wanted me to spill. "Well, the owner, Mr. Scalabrino, asked me to look at these properties. Not certain why. Maybe as investments."

Charlene wasn't fooled. "I see. Does he know that this area is just swimming with big department stores? Might want to look farther out the Tube loop."

"Tube loop?"

"The Underground. That's the transport system. You'll get familiar with it, I suppose, if you spend any time here."

"OK. Well, anyway, Mr. Scalabrino likes this area and he mentioned these sites specifically, so I guess I'd better scope them out."

"So, what are your impressions of the apartment building?"

I wanted to be tactful, but I suppose my grimace gave her a clue. She laughed.

"Right. Well, there are other properties, if that's not your cup of tea."

"I need to compare the other building to it to get a feel for the alternative," I said.

"Tomorrow. I have another client coming in shortly. Can I drop you somewhere?"

Charlene suggested I eschew cabs and acquire a pass and a map for the Underground at Victoria Station, which was close to our hotel.

Close is a relative term. On the train ride into London from Gatwick, a helpful bloke asserted our hotel was "only a stone's throw" from Victoria.

It turned out to be three or four stones' throw. We found it after schlepping our luggage quite a few blocks, almost getting run over when crossing the street twice. It would take some time before we looked the right way, and I mean to the right instead of the left, before crossing.

To say Lena and I were disoriented upon arrival is no exaggeration. In addition to jet lag, we had to learn our way around a huge city while gathering intelligence for the big boss.

Gathering intelligence. That makes it sound somewhat like a spy mission, given subsequent events, it's not far off the mark.

While waiting for Lena to show up, I decided to make a couple of calls on the international cellphone Scalabrino's cousin and right-hand man, Joe T, had supplied. First call was to Emmie. It had been too long since I heard that mellifluous voice—almost 24 hours. I was having a severe case of the heartsick.

Emmie was a bit startled that I called so early. I had forgotten the six-hour time difference. But she was glad to hear from me and wanted to know all about London, since she had never been there. I told her what little I knew to that point and promised I would get pictures (note to self: buy a disposable camera) and call every day.

Then a report to Joe T, who was to receive all pertinent information we gathered. I told him the apartment building was a dump, to which his only response was, "That's too bad." More details would be forthcoming after Lena accessed the property records, I told him.

It was getting on past noon and, although my sleeping and eating patterns had been thrown a monkey wrench, I decided it would be useful to assimilate the rhythm of jolly olde England. Since I had no way of contacting Lena—they only supplied us with the one cellphone—it was every man for himself.

Just down the block was a Barclays Bank, where I exchanged the wad of cash Scalabrino had supplied for pound notes. Yikes. I had no idea how much difference there was in the currencies. My stack of four thousand dollars quickly became only three grand in quid.

Judicious use of funds was called for, but since Freddie wasn't around, that might be possible.

All I had heard before heading overseas was: "Try the fish 'n' chips." That fare was available at "any pub," I was assured, so I sought out the nearest one. It found me only a couple of blocks from the hotel, a corner spot called Edgingham's.

Unlike American bars, which proclaim their selection of beers in neon in the windows, this one had no such gaudy street view, simply tasteful white stucco surrounding windows framed by dark, weathered wood. I entered and found a vacant two-person table by the far wall.

"What'll it be, love?" a perky young waitress stood before me, hands on hips, smiling. She was wearing an apron smudged with various foodstuffs and had her brown hair up in a bun cinched with a pencil. A nice face and very slender frame. Cerise was stitched across the front of the apron.

"Do you have a menu?" I asked.

She laughed and sat in the vacant chair across from me. "Yank, eh?"

"Yes, I'm American. Just got here."

She frowned, then smiled again. "Here's the scoop, dear. Fish 'n' chips. It's our specialty."

"OK, well, what other sandwiches—"

"Fish 'n' chips. That's the lunch menu." She waited. "It's quite good."

"Oh, no doubt. I guess I'll have the fish 'n' chips, then."

"Something to drink?"

Ah, now this question was in my comfort zone. "Bitter ale, if you have it."

"If I have it," she said with a smirk. "Coming right up." She rose and headed toward the bar.

Activity around me was lively because the place was near capacity. Most tables had two or three occupants. I was the only loner, thanks to Lena. I'm certain the other patrons considered me a loser. I thought I caught one looking my way and snickering.

As I waited for lunch to arrive, I scribbled a few notes on the building. It was hard to conceive of that being a viable location, given the time and expense of turning it into a department store. But maybe those were minor considerations for Scalabrino, who always seemed to get his way.

When Cerise brought the fish 'n' chips, I asked for a second round of bitter. Too bad Freddie wasn't here, I thought. He would appreciate the dark, potent brew.

Then I started thinking about Tina, the other member of my investigative team, up until recently. Shortly before Christmas, she left the store and entered the police academy. Although I was sad to see her go, I well understood her desire to pursue a more fulfilling line of work. I was itching to do the same myself. I made a note to call her later and catch up.

My introduction to the classic British pub fare was a success. The cod was fried to perfection, the chips—french fries to us yanks—were well seasoned and just short of the crispy side, and the peas were nicely buttered with a bit of a hot aftertaste.

When Cerise arrived to clear the now-empty plate, she asked, "And for afters?"

"Beg pardon?"

She laughed. "Sorry. Forgot you were a yank. Afters...it's what you call dessert. We have a nice fairy cake."

I didn't know what that was, but it seemed tragic to plop something sweet on top of that heavily salted meal. "No, I'm fine. Just the check." She smiled and left, returning shortly with a small slip of paper. On it was written "£4.60—thank you, Cerise."

It hardly seemed enough. "You sure this is my check?"

"Yes, too high?"

"No, I think you undercharged."

She glanced toward the bar. "Chef's special. You won the free meal of the day." She smiled again and headed back to the bar. I left a five-pound note, then added a couple more. I couldn't do the math in my head but was hoping it was an adequate tip.

3

Since I had no way to contact Lena, I headed back to the hotel. She had left a message at the front desk to come up to her room. She was on the seventh floor, I was on the fifth.

"Come on in, Beers," she called when I knocked. I entered to see her inspecting an array of Harrods bags lined up across her bed.

"Looks like someone's on shopper's holiday," I observed.

"Research, chum," she replied. "Dat's da most amazin' stoah I evah seen!"

"Well, one day we'll be going through La Scala London, and maybe it will be that spectacular."

"Doubt it," she deadpanned.

"I hope you didn't spend—"

"Don't worry, Beers. I got my own money." She pulled a shoebox out of a bag and dangled a pair of sparkling blue high heels for my perusal. "Like dat?"

"Very nice. But what...how is this research?"

"Jus' leave dat ta me. My depawtment." She continued pulling items out of other bags—a spaghetti-strap blue dress to match the shoes, a pair of blouses, a spangly necklace, a chunky metal bracelet and other accessories. Dollar signs were ringing up in my head, followed quickly by pound notes. I could vividly hear Pink Floyd playing "Money."

"Looks like you're planning for a catered affair."

"Naw, girls jus' gotta look good. I might hafta go check out Paris fa a coupla days." She continued inspecting her gear. "So what's fa lunch?"

"I already had lunch. I would have called you but there's the little matter of me having the only phone."

23

"S'OK. I had a bagel at Harrods."

We discussed plans for the rest of the day. Lena wanted to go through the packet of material provided by the estate agent, make notes, maybe follow up with some computer research in the hotel's business center. We agreed to meet for dinner later.

Until we got a look at the other property, there was little I could accomplish. So I decided a bit of exploration was in order.

When Johnny Scalabrino informed me he was sending me to London, my first thought was: music! This is where the bulk of my mammoth collection originated, starting with the British Invasion of the '60s, so it might be fertile ground for acquisitions. With a little time on my hands, I was eager to hunt and gather.

The guy manning the front desk was no help in my quest for a used record store, but a bellhop overheard and suggested I head down to Portobello Road, an area of eclectic shops and frequent rummage sales

It was time to learn my way around the city, and I had the incentive to do it. Trekking over to Victoria Station, I studied the Tube map and determined my route. Fortunately, it's all color-coded so it was a simple matter of riding the yellow line to Notting Hill Gate.

The area was as depicted. Retro clothing shops cheek by jowl with bric-a-brac vendors, snuggled against incense merchants, tea rooms, art galleries, antiques shops and pubs. It had a bit of everything, including a couple of record shops, where I pored through stacks of wax looking for that diamond among the coal heaps. I didn't find it.

At one shop called Mercy Beats, I met a girl with blue hair, Jillian. I gave her a general idea of what I was looking for, and she pointed me to the racks of oldies. When I didn't find anything that was missing from my personal compilation, I left my card with her, wrote the cell number on it and asked her to call me if she acquired anything rare in the next few days.

"So you're a collector, eh?" she said.

"I have a few things. Takes up a wall in my apartment. And a spare bedroom."

"I see."

"It's a hobby. At least right now it is."

"You should meet me uncle," Jillian said.

"Uncle?"

"Yeah, 'e were a right collector 'imself. 'ad every one-off there were."

"I'm sorry...I..."

"Used to be a deejay."

"Oh...I see. I'd love to take a look at his collection."

Jillian looked me over for a minute. "I'll ask him," she said, then went off to help a customer.

My hopes had been raised by the prospect of poring through a trove of long-forgotten recordings, discovering a slew of unique additions to my collection. But perhaps I appeared too eager and spooked Jillian. She had given me an odd look before attending to business.

After a pit stop in a pub for a pint, I continued down the road, through the residential area, where the inhabitants had opened their garages for rummage sales. Here's where the real action was. There was more opportunity than I had funds for, but I managed to walk away with some treasures the owners didn't realize they had: a still-sealed copy of the Small Faces' first album and an almost-mint 45 of "Paint It Black" by the Stones.

Fresh from my successful quest and still much of the afternoon ahead of me, I decided to head back toward the hotel on foot and see what the sights brought. Passing by Kensington Gardens and the palace, I soon came upon the Royal Albert Hall, the historic concert arena that hosted the Beatles, Jimi Hendrix, The Who and countless other acts. The current program, however—a Beatles tribute band—didn't appeal to me.

A few blocks away, the Victoria and Albert Museum featured a British invasion retrospective. It pulled me in. I saw the "fab gear" worn by those moptops of the '60s, along with some albums in glass cases that I wished I could add to my collection. Herman's Hermits, Gerry and the Pacemakers, the Yardbirds, the Dave Clark Five and, of course, the Beatles were well represented in photos, memorabilia and clips of TV appearances. I could have spent the rest of my London visit walking through that exhibit, but the boss might have objected. Besides, it was almost time to go to dinner with Lena, so I reluctantly headed back to the hotel.

When I knocked on her door at 7, Lena was ready, wearing a long, slinky black dress that showed a tasteful amount of cleavage. Plus the bangles she had acquired at Harrods earlier in the day. I surmised pub food wouldn't be appropriate and headed to my room to change.

As we were waiting for a cab—hiking to the Tube station wouldn't do in Lena's dolled-up condition—I asked where we were going.

"Harring's Heath."

"What's that?"

"British coo-zine. 'Sposta be good. Hadda hard time gettin' a resuhvation on a Friday evenin.' "

That gave me pause. The good restaurants were probably booked well in advance. If Lena was able to get a table at this one...well, it made me wonder. But I was willing to give it the benefit of the doubt.

The cabbie dropped us in the theater district, a couple of blocks off the Strand. This was another part of the city I wanted to explore. Seeing one of the current productions seemed another essential element of the London experience.

After some initial trepidation on my part, the meal turned out to be delicious beyond my expectations. Of the British fare offered, the steak and kidney pie appeared to be the most appealing, and I chose wisely. Lena opted for something called Steak Balmoral and Yorkshire pudding, which she also enjoyed, according to the number of pleased moans I heard her utter as she took bites.

In between nibbles, we managed to plan our schedule for the next few days. In the morning, a tour of the second building. Afternoon, Lena would hit the library archives to see what she could find out about the history of the two locations. I would visit the Daily Mail and try to find clippings. A trip to the property records office would have to wait until Monday, so Sunday would be free play day. Lena agreed to join me for tours of the Tower of London and Buckingham Palace.

Although we were both stuffed, we felt obligated to sample a dessert and settled for something called a "trifle." One taste was all I could manage and it was indeed good. Lena, despite admitting being completely full, finished off most of it.

As an introduction to London, I'd say it was a great success. I had some nice meals and found additions to my musical assembly. Lena scored on the shopping front.

Aside from the disappointing tour through Site Number One, it was a fine day to be in Jolly Olde England.

4

Saturday, April 7

That was our first day. Pretty uneventful, actually sort of fun. It quickly went downhill after that.

April in London is generally a delight. Temperatures are in the 40s, which the locals think is cold. That's not cold. Come to Minnesota and we'll show you cold. Forty is balmy, old chap, springlike.

However, my sinuses didn't appreciate the change in climate as much as the rest of me did. They went haywire, probably due to the higher humidity. I slogged through with the aid of sinus pills.

That didn't stop me from chugging beer at every opportunity.

Let's see, where was I? Oh, yes. So the second morning we got a look at the other property under consideration. Charlene McAllen met us at the site, on Knightsbridge, not far from Harrods, closer to Harvey Nichols. It was an ideal location, a little farther down the road than the first property but still well within the main shopping district.

The five-story building looked more suitable for occupation by a store right off the bat. In its most recent incarnation, it had been a warehouse for an import-export company. Charlene briefly outlined the history of the structure while leading us through the ground floor. The building was renovated numerous times, the last instance occurring in the '70s, she said.

"Most of the uppers are closed off for the moment," she explained. "We need to get the building inspector out to let us through the rest of the building. I have him on schedule for Monday.

"As you can see, high ceilings—very high—on the ground floor. It's a sharp..."

"Excuse me?" I interjected.

"A sharp. It's what the owner used to call this space."

"I don't get it."

"Well...the traditional living space, what you yanks call apartments, are flats in Britain. This being non-traditional, with a double-high ceiling—he called it a sharp. He had a weird sense of humor at that. I believe he was some sort of amateur musician."

"Oh, I see."

"And the other levels have high ceilings also. Not quite so high, though. Then there's a basement, where your power station is located."

"Da boilah 'n' such," Lena said.

"Quite so. And the lift mechanism is accessed there and at the roof."

We walked around the floor, which included one huge open space, punctuated by supporting pillars, and a back room in one corner divided into several offices. The front facing Knightsbridge had a row of large picture windows, almost floor to ceiling high. There were no windows in the side walls.

"The family are very keen to sell so I'm certain we can come to an accommodation," Charlene said. "We can go up to the first floor now, if you like."

"First floor?" I asked. "This isn't the first floor?"

"Oh, sorry, it's what you call the second floor. This is the ground floor."

Confusing, those British. Charlene led the way up. It was much like the first, only a more normal height ceiling. Unlike the first level, which had a concrete floor, this one featured well-worn wooden slats.

Again, we were hit with a strong odor, much like in the previous building we toured. This time, however, it was even stronger.

"Apologies again," Charlene said. "Normally this isn't a problem. You're just lucky, I guess." She laughed.

The intensity of the smell grew stronger as we walked the hall and approached a closed door.

"Behind there," I pointed. Lena looked at me, eyebrows raised, as if to ask, should we disturb the occupant? We had a job to do, so it was imperative that we at least look at the room. My notes wouldn't be complete unless we did.

I nodded to Charlene and she slowly opened the door. "Hello? Are you there?"

No answer came and, to our relief the room was empty. The scent actually seemed better inside. The room gave way to some inner offices, all vacant. Charlene indicated the "fragrance" could just be due to a minor plumbing problem.

We checked a couple more rooms and were about to wind up the "first floor" tour. The last door we opened was the killer. The stink hit our olfactory senses like a sledge hammer. This office wasn't vacant. In the corner was a bundle of rags, with someone underneath. Unlike the last time, however, no snore was issued.

We moved a bit closer to see whether there were signs of breathing. "Got a bad feelin' bout dis, cap," Lena whispered.

"I'll check on him," Charlene said. She shook a corner of the covered figure. No movement. Cautiously, she lifted the top blanket a smidgeon and peered underneath.

I saw the blood immediately and was about to yell "Wait!" when Charlene let out a screech and backed away quickly. Lena didn't want any part of the scene and promptly exited the room.

"Is he...?" Charlene started.

I shrugged. The flavor in the air indicated "street person," but it could just as well have been "body in decomposition." Only one way to find out whether we needed an ambulance or the meat wagon. I ventured forward, holding my breath, and lifted the cover. No question—this man was very dead.

He looked middle-aged, with a scruffy beard and pug nose. The most significant identifying feature was a deep, bloodied crease from above his right eye at the scalp line and across the bridge of his nose. It was obviously the source of the pool of blood around his head. The neck of a bottle was protruding from the blanket at his chest.

Charlene dialed the police, and we retreated to the ground floor to await their arrival. She was flabbergasted. "This is not the norm, I assure you," she said. "I have no idea what's going on right now. Social services are normally on top of the situation."

I tried to reassure her that every big city has a homeless population, and they are always at risk of something. However, I refrained from relating the sordid history of my recent encounters with murder. This had no bearing on the assignment—or so I thought at the time.

The police came, surveyed the situation, summoned the coroner and asked us a few questions. The constable in charge speculated that the deceased had wandered into the building to drink, had too much and staggered into the door frame, where he sliced open his head and bled to death. He said these types of things are an all-too-frequent occurrence, indicating one or two of the down-and-out turned up missing or dead per month. "Hard lot to police," he concluded.

"Got any more bums we can check on?" Lena asked sarcastically.

"I am so, so sorry," Charlene said. Since we couldn't see the rest of the building until the inspector came around, there was little else we could do there. Charlene offered to make it up to us by inviting us to dinner with her and her husband Sunday at a restaurant in the theater district.

As we headed to the Tube, Lena and I discussed whether there was any further research we could complete during the weekend. Our schedule included a trip to the library archives for her and the newspaper for me. After a short discussion, we determined this site was already highly qualified, compared with the other building. Even with the body count.

We decided to blow off the research and start our sightseeing a day early, beginning with the Tower of London. Our Beefeater guide was highly entertaining and elicited gasps from the crowd as he described the process of beheading criminals housed in the tower.

The crown jewels whetted Lena's appetite for royal trappings. While inching past the orbs, sceptres, tiaras and impossibly large diamonds, Lena whispered to me, "Doze are fake, ya know."

"I don't think so," I replied.

"You think they'd put deze priceless things on display, where any Tom, Dick 'n' Jane could snatch 'em?"

"They're pretty well guarded," I said.

"I know my jewry," she responded, "and I say dey fake."

Naturally, Lena wanted to follow up with a tour through Buckingham Palace. I figured the concept of royalty was a novelty she wanted to explore further. This time, however, she oohed and aahed at the treasures on display. "Da real thing," she whispered. I didn't see the difference, but Lena handled jewelry all day, so I reckoned she had a better idea about that stuff than I did.

I suggested we hit a pub on the way back to the hotel for an early dinner before resting up for more sightseeing on Sunday. We popped into Edgingham's, and this time I had a better idea about what to expect. Cerise was on duty again and brought over menus for our inspection.

"Welcome back," she said, handing me one.

"No need for that," I said. "Fish 'n' chips for me. And the bitter."

"What dey got heah dat's good?" Lena asked while looking up and down the menu. Cerise raised her eyebrows, first at Lena, then at me.

"She's from New Orleans," I explained.

"Ah," Cerise said. "Wonderful accent. I suggest the Wellington, love."

"What's dat?" Lena asked.

"Tenderloin wrapped in prosciutto, shallots, garlic, mushrooms, butter..."

"Ya got me at prosciutto, love. I'll try dat." She handed the menu back.

"Wait," I stopped Cerise from walking off. "I thought you said fish 'n' chips was the specialty?"

"That's lunch, dear. Check the clock." She left to turn in the order.

"You been heah before?" Lena asked.

"Yesterday, while you were shopping."

"Waitress is cute," she said, giving me a "go for it" leer.

I rolled my eyes. "If you recall, I have a girlfriend," I retorted. Which reminded me I needed to call Emmie and update her on our progress. "Be right back," I said, heading out the door.

On the corner, I dialed Emmie's number. It was still morning back in Minnesota, while the day was drawing to a close in London, a time difference I was having trouble getting adjusted to.

"Hey, sweetie. What's happening?"

"Hi, Jim. Good to hear from you. Nothing going on here. Same old same old. You having fun?"

No need to alarm her with our grim discovery. "A little. Not much work getting done over the weekend. So we're doing some tourist stuff—Tower of London, Buckingham Palace. I went to the Victoria and Albert Museum yesterday. Pretty cool."

"Sounds like fun. Wish I could be there."

"Yeah, me too." Suddenly I was homesick. I wanted to be with Emmie, hold her and kiss her. But she was an ocean away. Although my persuasive powers had been on target lately, I couldn't manage to get her added to my entourage for the London gig.

"Well, take lots of pictures for me," she said.

"Oh, will do. I'm hoping we can wrap this up in the early part of the week and I can be home by Wednesday or Thursday." In retrospect, wishful thinking, or maybe I was just kidding myself.

"That sounds great. Keep in touch, Jim."

"Wait. I miss you so much…what are you wearing?"

She laughed. Then she told me she was naked, as usual. That led to some great visuals in my head and a vow to ravish her for hours on end upon my return. "Can't wait," she said breathlessly.

After we ended our naughty conversation, I headed back inside with a sinking feeling. There was joy and excitement at hearing Emmie's voice but sadness at realizing she was so far away. The next few days were going to drag by, I was certain, even with the prospect of exploring an exotic locale like London. With Emmie by my side, it would have been a total joy. Not that Lena was a drag, but it just wasn't the same.

"What do you want to do this evening?" I asked Lena as we finished up our dinner. "You interested in hearing some live music?"

"Beers, we don't gotta hang out all da time," she replied.

"I didn't imply that. I just thought—"

"You go do ya thing, and I'll find somethin' ta keep me busy." She gave me a sly grin. She was up to something. When we parted outside the restaurant, I had the suspicion she was on her way to do more retail "research."

So I had my own investigation to conduct, and it had nothing to do with stores or shopping. I was on a musical mission, and I determined to soak up as much of the London sound as time permitted.

At one of the record shops I had visited, I picked up a flyer announcing an exclusive engagement for the Pony Riders, a Jethro Tull tribute band. It was at a club just off the Tube, not far from the zoo. I had time for a couple hours of shuteye before heading out refreshed and ready for rocking out.

5

There is little of note to report of the evening's events. The club I visited was jam-packed with drinkers and smokers (there was a whiff of funny weed in the air). Only a few tables around the periphery, with the majority of the floor open for dancing and head-banging.

It was the kind of dive I imagined the Beatles got their start in—smoky, dimly lit, few decorations, a sticky floor, surly waitresses, bad acoustics. But the music was loud and crowd-pleasing, as the band whipped through a medley of Tull's early repertoire, including "Teacher," "With You There to Help Me," "Locomotive Breath" and "Thick as a Brick."

At one point a young lady approached me and smiled. Between songs I managed to place her because of her blue hair—the clerk I had met at the record shop, Jillian. She was dating the bass player and wanted to know what I thought. But the music resumed before I could offer my opinion, and she soon wandered off.

I have no idea what Lena was up to that evening. She can be secretive, but I was hard pressed to imagine her doing what I was doing. More likely, she was attending an opera or continuing her shopping blitz.

DRAGGING MYSELF out of bed late Sunday morning, I managed to catch the tail end of the traditional English breakfast buffet in the hotel's dining room: sausage, baked beans, stewed tomatoes, mushrooms, fried potatoes, poached eggs. Seemed like an odd combo to me, but when in Britain...

Lena wandered down even later than me and settled for a cup of coffee and piece of toast with marmalade. She looked half-asleep.

When I inquired about her evening, she mumbled, "S'awright," then declined when I suggested we visit more tourist attractions that day. Once again, flying solo.

As I was leaving, I touched her left shoulder and she cringed.

"What's the matter?" I asked.

"Hurts," she said.

"How did you hurt it?"

She just shook her head. I shrugged and left.

As I was getting ready to head out, I formulated a game plan that included more music shops and a return to the garage sales down Portobello Road. I was determined to do whatever I could to fill in the gaps in my collection in this fertile area. The prospect of scoring some rare imports danced in my head.

Also, I wanted to explore more of the traditional must-see sites—the British Museum, Westminster Abbey, Big Ben, the Tate, London Bridge. They were all easily accessible by Tube. Since I had no clue when I'd ever get back to London, it seemed imperative to fulfill my duties as a first-time visitor.

My persistence on the musical front was rewarded when, just after a lunch break for fish 'n' chips and a pint of bitter, as I was digging through about my 50th box of the day, I came across a still shrink-wrapped eight-track tape of The Who's *Tommy*. The price was one pound. Who said a pound wouldn't buy anything nowadays?

Only much later, as I was strolling across a bridge to get a better photo of Big Ben, did the incident at breakfast start to worry me. How did Lena hurt her shoulder? Had she bumped into something hard, maybe while she was shopping and not paying attention? Then I thought what if she had fallen down and hurt herself? I didn't see any other visible bruises or scrapes.

Could she have been mugged? It's not entirely impossible, seeing as we were in a strange city and could easily wander into an unsafe area. Although we had pretty much stuck to the central part of London, which seemed totally secure. At least I had. Where had Lena gone last night?

As my brain is wont to do, it began concocting all sorts of scenarios in which Lena was imperiled and suffered injury. My reasoning side told me this was needless worry, that there was a simple explanation for it. But my worrywart side insisted that I grill Lena about it at the next opportunity.

I managed to cross all the museums off my list of things to see by blitzing through them at light speed. It was information overload but all very interesting. Still, the music exhibit at Victoria and Albert was more intriguing than anything I subsequently saw, and I determined I would revisit it before leaving town.

Lena didn't answer when I dialed her room, so I left a message telling her when to be ready for our dinner date. I had one really nice set of clothes, outside my normal getup of black T-shirt and black jeans, and I was sporting that as I met Lena at the curb to wait for Charlene and her husband to pick us up.

Lena was dazzling. She had on a fine black velvet dress with long sleeves and a split up the side. My meager gray slacks and green polo made me feel underdressed.

"You look nice," I said. "New dress?"

"Thanks. Yeah, found dis on da sale rack at Debenhams."

"What about that blue dress you showed me?"

She hesitated. "Dudn't work. May hafta take it back."

It was hard for me to imagine Lena looking bad in anything, but I remembered it was a spaghetti-strap number. Did she want to conceal her shoulder injury?

As I was about to inquire with all the subtlety I could muster, Charlene and her husband pulled to the curb and she called a toodle-oo. We got in the back and sped off toward the restaurant.

Charlene turned sideways from the front seat. "Jim, Lena, this is my husband, A.J."

"How do?" he said.

"Hi," I said.

"Glad ta meet ya," Lena added.

"Hope you chaps are enjoying our fair town," he said.

"Very educational," I replied. I glanced at Lena but she remained silent.

"We're taking you to one of our favorite places," Charlene said. "Little restaurant called BritSquire. Fabulous dishes." She beamed at us.

A.J. dropped us off at the front and went to park. Our table was waiting for us in the middle of the dining room with a nice view of traffic through the bustling theater district.

When A.J. arrived at the table, I got my first real look at his attire and then I felt overdressed. He had on jeans, some sort of sports jersey and a well-worn jacket over it. Looked like he was ready to hop on a fishing boat.

"I must say, you look lovely, Lena," Charlene said.

"Thanks," she said. "Been doin' some shoppin' round heah. Lotsa bawgains." She winked at Charlene, who giggled and nodded.

"Shall we go a round of drinks?" A.J. asked. He signaled a waiter and we ordered: wine for the ladies, scotch rocks for A.J. and more bitter ale for me.

"So, Charlene tells me you're from Minnesota," A.J. said.

"Well, we live there," I responded. "Not from there originally."

"New Awlins," Lena said.

"New Orleans Saints?" A.J. asked. Lena nodded. "Saints fan myself," he replied, opening his jacket to show off his jersey. "Northampton Saints, that is," he said with a grin.

"Rugby team," Charlene explained. "A.J. played for them for a season."

"Now, dear, I think 'played' is an exaggeration," A.J. replied. "Traveling squad. Glorified bench warmer." He laughed.

Drinks came, menus were distributed and Charlene offered to order for us. "You won't be disappointed," she said. "Is there anything you won't eat?" Lena and I looked at each other, then shrugged. "Ah, good. I have just the thing in mind, if you don't mind sharing." Shrugs again. "Great."

The waiter was summoned and she ordered something called Round the Molly, plus a couple of appetizers.

I'm not certain what it was that we were eating, but Charlene allowed that it was a concoction of prawns, sweetbreads and other mystery ingredients served over rice. It was too thick for gumbo and there wasn't any okra, so far as I could tell, but on the whole, it was scrumptious. Lena had seconds and I went for a dab of thirds from the big ceramic tureen in the middle of the table.

After the meal, as we were sipping cognac—Lena opted for coffee and apple pie—I asked where else we could sample this dish, figuring we'd find a nice restaurant close to the hotel. A.J. said this was the specialty of BritSquire, and we couldn't find it elsewhere. "And it's only available by request," he added.

On the ride back, Charlene reminded us about our appointment in the morning to meet with the building inspector at the warehouse site. I felt fairly certain we could also wrap up our research on Monday and be winging our way back home on Tuesday.

Wrong again, mojumbo.

6

Monday, April 9

For some reason, the building inspector required that we be present when he arrived at the ungodly hour of 7:30 in the morning. I was unsure whether this was his regular schedule or it was just a case of torture the jetlagged yanks.

At any rate, we skipped breakfast and arrived only a few minutes late as he and Charlene were chatting near the entrance.

"Jim, Lena, this is Roddy Jemson."

"Hello," he said, extending his hand. We shook and made small talk for a few minutes before heading in. Jemson had a clipboard containing a sheaf of papers, including a diagram of each floor and a checklist, which he constantly referred to as he made notes and mumbled through the levels.

"Of course, the lift needs a proper inspection by a certified engineer, which I won't do today," he explained, as we took stairs to the second level.

Jemson made notes on everything—the walls, the floors, the light fixtures, the windows. He skipped the plumbing for the moment since water service had been shut off some time previously, but he tested every light and outlet.

On the second floor, or first floor if you're British, the odor had dissipated from the room where we discovered the derelict. Thank goodness.

The third floor was divided into offices and cubicles. Only one office had a desk and chairs. On the wall was a calendar from August 1994. It had been unoccupied for quite a while, apparently. Charlene mentioned that the owners used to play hide and seek in these offices as children.

From there we went straight up to the rooftop, where Jemson advised us to wait in the stairwell for a moment. He checked something or other, then let us walk out and look around.

"Wow, nice view," Lena gushed, heading for the front precipice. My fear of heights kept me well away from the short retaining wall around the perimeter.

My mind drifted immediately to another London rooftop scene, the farewell concert the Beatles staged in conjunction with the release of *Let It Be*.

When Lena leaned over the wall and exclaimed, "Look at all a dem shoppahs!" I hightailed it back to the stairwell to wait. No sense fainting on the roof.

In time, they returned and we walked into the top level, empty except for an enormous clock on the south wall and a large cardboard box in the middle of the floor. The clock was stopped at 2:13. The box contained several open and mostly empty cans of paint, none of which looked like it matched the walls.

Jemson only peeked in from the stairwell on four, then headed straight down to the basement. After wandering around for a while, he announced that the boiler would need a full cycling and checkup when the water was turned back on, and the phone panel would need to be replaced entirely.

"And the electrical circuits are underpowered," he declared. "Nowadays, we like to see something with a bit more juice. Plan to add computers?"

I nodded.

"Yes, well, I didn't see any network ports, so that will all need to be retrofitted. Unless, of course, you plan to use the building as a warehouse again." He raised his eyebrows.

"No, sir. Not a warehouse," I said. "What about all those posts on each floor?"

"Load-bearing. They stay as is. You have the blueprints?"

I looked at Charlene and she shook her head.

"Apparently not."

"Contact my office and you can purchase a set. Or you can get the owners to provide a set when the bill of sale is signed." He handed me a card, then bid us adieu.

"Well, what do you think?" Charlene asked after he left.

"I like it," Lena said.

"Looks usable as a department store, more so than the other place," I said.

"And the price is negotiable, I'm fairly certain," Charlene offered.

"I don't know anything about pricing," I said. "We're just supposed to figure out whether it's possible to make a store out of the building."

"Well then...marvelous!" Charlene said. "I suppose you'll be recommending this location. I'll have my office write up the purchase agreement and fax it to...?" She raised her eyebrows at me.

I looked at Lena. "We still have a little more information to gather but...sure, I'll get you a number. I'll have to check in with my folks."

"Splendid. Well, is there anything else I can show you? Need directions to the building inspector's office? Do you need a recommendation on a restaurant?" she said with a laugh.

"No, I think we can take it from here," I said. "I'll get that fax number to you tomorrow." Charlene locked up the building, we shook and she headed off to her next appointment.

"Think dey gonna buy it, cap?" Lena asked.

"I don't see why not. If it's between this place and the apartment building, there's no contest. This will need a bit of renovation, sprucing up, but nothing like what the other one would require. Scalabrino could get this store open in a year's time, I imagine."

"Renuhvation? How much you figure dat's gonna cost?"

"Well...I have no idea."

"Maybe dey want us ta get some idea while we heah."

I thought about this and decided Lena was right. "I'll check in with Joe T and see what he thinks."

It was still morning when we finished up, which meant it was the wee hours back in Minneapolis. Might be better to wait and call later on, I decided. I suggested we grab an early lunch, then do some sightseeing to kill time. Lena agreed that was a capital idea. She wanted to take a tour of London on a double-decker bus, which sounded like it might be fun.

We grabbed a bite on the run and headed to Trafalgar Square, starting point for the ride, which turned out to be great fun. Riding above the traffic in an open-air seating area, we passed by most of the highpoints of the London experience: Buckingham Palace, the Tower of London and London Bridge, Parliament and Big Ben, Fleet Street, Westminster Abbey, Hyde Park and the like.

Lena struck up a conversation with a couple who turned out to be from New Orleans. She recognized the accent right away, and they quickly got up to speed on each other's history.

The Wilsons were on a 40th anniversary tour of the British Isles, their first trip across the Atlantic, like us. Turned out their daughter went to school in Harahan with Lena's cousin. Small world. They spent quite a bit of time discussing the prospects of the New Orleans football team in the draft.

At the end of the tour, Lena asked if they wanted to go to dinner, but they declined. They were catching a train to Brighton to make a circuit of the country along the coast. They exchanged email addresses and promised to stay in touch.

"What are the odds?" I asked Lena as we headed back to the hotel.

"Doncha know we everywayah?"

"People from New Orleans?" I asked.

"Saints fans," she replied.

During the tour, I noticed that Lena grimaced when another passenger bumped into her left arm. I decided to inquire again about it.

"Is everything OK?" I asked.

"Whatcha mean?"

"With your arm. Did you hurt it?"

Lena stared at me a beat, looked down, then said, "I met a guy."

Visions of a thug wearing leather who beat her flashed through my mind. I was imagining all sorts of dangerous scenarios.

She sighed. "Let's hit dat pub. It's a long story."

7

E dgingham's was deserted at that time of day. Too late for lunch, too early for dinner. It was Cerise's day off so we had a new waitress who seemed decidedly less friendly. We took the hint and ordered fish 'n' chips without the chit-chat. Lena had a soft drink, but I needed a beer.

When the drinks arrived, Lena started into her tale. She was shopping at Fenwick on Bond Street, another of the posh department stores. As she was perusing the women's shoes, another customer, a sharply attired gentleman in a dark gray suit, started making small talk.

His name was Charles Fulham. He said he was looking for a pair of shoes for his wife's birthday, something sensational, so he could take her out dancing. He noticed that Lena was very nicely dressed and thought she had similar tastes in clothing.

Lena said she was happy to oblige and pointed out several possibilities before Fulham decided on a pair of sequined black high heels. He was so appreciative of her assistance that he offered to buy her a drink and wouldn't take no for an answer.

"He also thought I had a cute accent," she said with a smile. "Told him he was da one wit' da accent."

They hit a pub in Marylebone, as it turns out not far from the club where I was, and they had a cordial drink. Then one more as Fulham had called his wife and invited her down to join them.

Lena and the wife, Mary Clare, hit it off, seeing as they both were into clothes and she was also from the States. Fulham presented the shoes, Mary Clare loved them, Lena got the credit, yada yada yada, more rounds were bought.

Mary Clare insisted that Lena drink something called a Purple Stripe. She had no clue what was in it but is pretty sure it knocked her on her ass. The rest of the night was fuzzy, she said, but she woke up with a sore shoulder.

"An' heah's why," Lena said. "First, promise you won't laugh."

I quickly promised. An injury wasn't a laughing matter in my mind; I was concerned for her well-being.

She rolled up her sleeve.

I gaped. Then I burst out laughing—I couldn't help myself.

"You bastahd," Lena said.

"I'm sorry," I managed between guffaws, "but you're the last person I would expect..." My side started to hurt from laughing.

Lena's cold stare slowly started to melt as I continued roaring. In time, she was smiling.

"Awright, awright. Funny. I know," she said. "Like you nevah totally screwed up."

Wiping my eyes, I managed to get myself under control, took a few deep breaths and asked, "How did that happen?"

I stared at the Union Jack on her shoulder in amazement.

"Demon rum," Lena said, shaking her head. "Aftah dat drink, I'm not sure what happened, but it musta been a visit to a tattoo parlah. I hadda be outta my mind ta do dis." She rolled down her sleeve.

"I'm pretty sure you can get those erased nowadays."

She perked up at this. "Yeah? How?"

"Not certain, but I think they can do it. Laser something or other."

"I'm gonna research dat right now. See ya latah," she said, scurrying off.

Then the waitress brought the food. I informed her that the other party had an emergency and had to leave, so I'd need the food as takeouts. She frowned and took the plates away.

This certainly wasn't like the Lena I knew. She was very proper and always in control. But maybe there was a side of her I didn't know about. After all, she was a Gemini. Perhaps the devil side of her twin personality made her do it in her drunken stupor.

I brought the dinners back to the hotel, but Lena wasn't in her room. She was obviously off somewhere doing her computer research, probably at a library. Oh well. My fish 'n' chips were superb. I left hers in my mini-fridge.

I planned to report to Joe T around noon Minneapolis time, which meant I had some hours to waste before my call. The business center in the lobby was vacant, so I fired up the computer. The front desk clerk helped me log in and locate a word processor. I scanned my notes and tried to organize them into a coherent report, and in short order I had my executive summary printed out. It was rather terse, only four pages, but it got to the point and recommended the second site.

There was still a bit of time to kill, so I decided to down a few pints at a corner table in the lobby bar. Lena wandered in and spotted me shortly before 6, beaming.

"Did you find something?" I asked.

"Yep, got a lazah centah in Brooklyn Pawk. Dey can take it off."

I ordered her a celebratory glass of white wine.

"Jus' one," she said firmly.

At the appointed hour, I called Joe T. He was on his way out to lunch with some of the mansion staff—Scalabrino's goons, as Tina always referred to them—but he had time to hear the report, which I skimmed through and hit the highlights.

"So, bottom line, you think this place is suitable?" he asked.

"Absolutely."

"You get a sales contract for us to look at?"

"The estate agent is going to fax that over," I said. "She just needs the fax number." He gave it.

"And what about renovation costs? Painting, refinishing floors, installing fixtures, wiring and so on?"

"I don't know."

"Well, find out. Johnny has a rehab specialist that he works with in London...hold on." I heard him put the phone down, then return a minute later. "Garry Naughton. He did the London house."

"London house?" I asked.

"Yeah, Johnny's London house."

"I didn't know he had a house here."

"Well now you do. So call him and tell him this is for Johnny, and we need it done pronto." He gave me the number.

"Got it."

"Lena doing OK?" he asked.

I glanced at her, sipping her wine. "Yeah, she's fine. She's going to spend tomorrow looking up the property records on the building. We can also get a set of blueprints from the building inspector's office."

"Good. OK, gotta go get some lunch. Call me tomorrow." He hung up.

"I need to meet with a renovation specialist tomorrow while you're researching."

"No problemo," Lena said.

I dialed Garry Naughton and left a message. Then I called Charlene and left another message. With any luck, they would call me back and get this rolling.

"By the way, your lunch is in my fridge. You want it?"

"Stawvin'," she replied. "Let's go." We headed up, I gave her the takeout box and she dug into it cold as she headed up to her room.

I called Emmie for my daily fix of sweet-talking. Nothing new to report at the store; all quiet on the western front. I brought her up to speed on our next step and opined that I should be home before the end of the workweek. She was happy to hear that.

Oh, by the way, she said, Tina called and sounded frantic, wanted my number. So did Freddie. I had instructed Emmie not to give out my number in London, and she was holding up her end of the bargain. I said I'd give them a ring.

As I was about to dial Tina, Garry Naughton called and said he would meet me at the site at 11 Tuesday morning. I dialed Charlene again and asked her to be at the building to open it at that time.

Then a call to Tina, who whispered, "Can't talk now. Call you back in a few." I gave her the number, but no callback ensued.

Freddie didn't answer his office number, so he was either out on assignment or having a three-beer lunch. I left a message saying I'd try him again on Tuesday. For a fraction of a second, I thought about giving him the number, but quickly rejected that idea as foolish.

8

Tuesday, April 10

This was our last workday in London, I thought, as we enjoyed a leisurely English breakfast. Then Lena headed off to do research, and I took the Tube to the building site.

I was a bit early and enjoyed walking through the busy blocks, watching pedestrians and motorists, getting a feel for the beat of the city. It was a great town, one I would love to share with someone special in a non-work setting. Very quickly, I decided it would take quite a bit of savings to come back with Emmie on my own dime.

The weather had turned suddenly cooler after an overnight shower, so I sported one of my few concessions to fashion on this trip, a brown tweed jacket. As 11 approached, I headed to the warehouse to wait for Charlene and Garry Naughton. Near the front door, a man in bib overalls holding a briefcase was looking up and down the sidewalk.

"Mr. Naughton?" I asked.

"Garry Naughton," he said, extending his hand.

"Jim Biersovich."

"This the building?"

"Yes. It's an empty warehouse and Mr. Scalabrino—"

"You work for him?" he asked.

"Uh-huh. I'm chief of security for the chain."

"What chain?"

"La Scala."

"Sorry, what's that?"

"Department stores. Johnny owns five stores in the U.S. and this will be—"

"Oh, I see. I thought he was looking for another apartment." This time I was confused.

Naughton explained that Scalabrino owned a house just outside London and an apartment in Chelsea, both of which he renovated.

We chit-chatted a bit more, waiting for Charlene to show up with the key. Naughton kept checking his watch, so I decided I'd better make a call. There was no answer at her office so I assumed she was on the way. After another half-hour, we decided she had either forgotten about it or had been otherwise delayed.

"Not sure what to do here," I said. "I've left several messages."

"Just as well. The architect couldn't make it today anyway," he said. "If you get it set up again, give me a call." Then he left.

Before I followed his example, I stuck a card in the door with a note that we'd missed her and she should call me when she showed up.

It was getting on to noon, and Lena said she would call around then to see if I was up for lunch. When she rang, she reported she was at the University of Westminster on Regent Street, just a few Tube stops away. We agreed to meet at a corner and pick one of the many eateries in the area.

Over a green pepper and olive pizza, we exchanged updates. Lena was surprised Charlene didn't show or even call; something must be wrong, she guessed. Duh. That was my guess also.

"Found a lotta propuhty transactions in da books," she said. "Dat site was 'riginally owned by da Earl a Wainwright. He also owned da site a Harrods but nevah built on it."

Lena iterated the transitions of the property, from livery to high-traffic saloon and cathouse, a fire that leveled the place, then reconstruction as a general merchandise store with an upper level for living quarters and storage.

In the late 1800s, it once again succumbed to fire and was rebuilt, this time as a six-story apartment building. Then conversion to office space in the early 1910s, with a bank at street level, followed by transition to a warehouse after World War II, then a major renovation in the 1950s that combined the first and second floors, when it briefly served as an auto dealership and law offices, followed by reversion to warehouse space before finally closing in the 1990s.

"Da family dat has owned it since da '70s is da Featherstonaughs. Dey got an address in Luton, wherevah dat is."

"Wonder why they want to sell now?"

"Dunno, but I 'spect it's cuz dey weren't makin' money wit' da wayahhouse."

"You finished with the research then?" I asked.

"Naw, gotta go ta da inspectah's office an' pick up da blueprints, den head ovah ta look at da Survey a London at da Bartlett School. You can tag along if ya want."

"No, that's OK. I need to track down Charlene McAllen and see what's going on. I've got to get this renovation estimate so we can get out of here."

"Anxious ta get back, are ya?" Lena smirked.

"I thought you were too because of...y'know," I responded, pointing to her shoulder.

She lost the smile. "Yeah. See ya latah."

The only number I had for Charlene was her cell, which she wasn't answering. But I had the address of the agency, so I inquired at a Tube station and got the general route to follow.

The office of Tilden Moncrief McAllen was just off the A11 near Queen Mary University. A closed sign was on the door, but I could see an older woman at a desk near the back wall. I rapped on the glass. She approached, shook her head and indicated the closed sign.

I held my card to the glass and said Charlene missed an appointment that morning, and I needed to get in touch with her. The woman hesitated a moment, then opened the door.

"Miss McAllen will be out for a while, I'm afraid."

"What? Why?"

She hesitated again before continuing. "Charlene was mugged last night. She's in hospital."

There are a few good reasons for missing an appointment, and this was certainly one of them. I was at a loss for words. The stunned look on my face prompted the woman to invite me in to sit down. She brought a cup of water while I tried to wrap my head around this development.

"Listen, Mr....Biersovich? Is that right?" she asked, taking the card from my hand.

"Yes," I said. "Call me Jim."

"Jim. I'm Trudy. Trudy James. I manage the office."

"So what do I do now?" I asked. "Is there another agent...?"

"Yes. Mr. Tilden has been notified. He's on his way back from Bristol, should arrive this evening."

It still seemed unreal, although this was the sort of thing that happened all the time. "Is she OK?"

"They're still running tests, so I don't...she had a bit of a..." Trudy had trouble putting it into words. She pointed to her head.

"Hit in the head?" I asked.

"Yes, just so. Or maybe she was knocked down and struck the pavement. We don't know all the details because she hasn't been able to say much. Mr. McAllen is with her." She wrung her hands.

I looked around the office, searching for what I didn't know. It occurred to me that I should go visit her. And that I should let Lena know as soon as possible. And somehow still get the mission accomplished.

"More water?"

Trudy's question woke me from my contemplation. "Miss James, I have a bit of a problem." I felt ill at ease but soldiered forward. "I'm embarrassed to bring this up what with Charlene...we were scheduled to look at a property this morning."

"I understand."

"I'm supposed to meet with an architect tomorrow and—"

"Oh, no question," she interrupted. "Just leave that to me. What was the property?"

I gave her the address, and she assured me that Tilden would be there to open the building or she would shut down the office and come herself. She just had to locate the key.

9

fter making arrangements once again to meet with the
renovator and architect, I stopped at Edgingham's on my
way back to the hotel. Since I had no way to contact Lena,
she was in the dark about this latest development. Nothing
I could do but wait for her to contact me, and have an adult
beverage while doing it.

Cerise was back on duty. She laughed when I said, "The usual,"
but she remembered my beer of preference and put in an order of
fish 'n' chips. It was a couple hours since the pizza, and I was
starving again. Must have been something in the air of London that
honed my appetite. I decided a few calls would pass the time until
the food arrived.

Of course, I started with Emmie. With Assignment: London on
the verge of wrapping up, assuming we could get the renovator in
and out in 24 hours, I was eager to get back to my girl.

"Good to hear your voice again," she said.

"You'll be hearing it in person soon, I hope."

"Are you finished there? When are you returning?"

"Almost finished. We've hit a bit of a snag. But I think we can
wrap this up tomorrow and book a flight either tomorrow evening
or Thursday. I would say Friday latest."

"What's the snag?"

"Our real estate agent got mugged."

"No!"

"Yeah, I should visit her in the hospital before I leave. We had
dinner with her and her husband the other night."

"Is she OK?"

"I guess so. Anyway, someone in her office will help us get our
last look tomorrow, and we should be able to pack up."

"Have you talked to Jane?" Jane Mertin, Emmie's boss, was head of facilities at La Scala.

"No. Should I?"

"I think you might want to call her."

"What's going on, Emmie?"

"There was a problem this morning. I don't have the details, but she's been in with Mr. Foster for quite a while."

"Shoplifting?"

"Worse. Armed robbery."

"Holy crap! Anybody hurt?"

"Not that I know of. But maybe you should give her a call."

"Thanks. I'll do that." I told Emmie how much I missed her and wished she was in London. She gave me that delightful laugh and said she missed me also. I again told her a couple of things I wanted to do with her when I returned. "You naughty boy!" she said with another laugh.

I dialed Salmon Foster's office and got his secretary, Candace, who said it was noisy in his office, but she would put me through.

"Biersovich! Where are you!"

"Still in London, sir."

"Yes, I knew that," he said, with a tone that indicated he had forgotten.

"Has there been a problem at the store?"

"We have it under control."

"Something about an armed robbery?"

He hesitated before answering. "Holdup right after opening. Robbers hit cosmetics and sportswear registers on the first floor and fled before the guards on duty could arrive. Didn't get much, just the starting till on four registers."

"Anyone able to identify them?"

"No, wore masks. Otherwise nondescript. At least to our scared shitless clerks."

"You probably need me back right away then," I said.

"No, Mr. Scalabrino is putting his team on it," Foster replied.

His "team" meant Detective Cuccia, the boss's friend on the police force, along with Scalabrino's mansion gang, whose exact duties I've never been able to figure out. My guess would be enforcers.

"OK. Well, let me know if you need me to catch the next flight back."

"You'll be the first to know," he said, hanging up.

Joe T was the next logical call.

"I heard about the problem at the store. Foster didn't seem to think I needed to come back yet."

"No, we've got it under control," Joe T said.

"Cuccia?"

"We're bringing in Roger Thompson, the Vegas guy."

I recalled that Thompson had quit after being suspected of involvement in a theft at the Las Vegas store. "I thought they hired that new woman, what's her name?"

"She didn't work out. They just brought Thompson back. Now we need him here while you're...preoccupied."

"Joe T, I can hop the next flight back."

"You finish with the site survey? Got the renovation estimate?"

"No, not yet. They'll do that tomorrow. But they can just email the estimate, right? I don't really need to be here."

"Yeah. You do. We've got it in hand. Take care of business there, and we'll do likewise here." He cut the connection.

Son of a bitch. There was little more I could do here. We had decided on the site, Lena was gathering all the background data, I had my notes, and the renovator would be by in the morning to look it over and work on an estimate.

And an interloper was doing my job back home. London was nice and all, but I was extremely eager to get back to home base and within the proximity of Emmie's warming aura.

Cerise brought the fish 'n' chips, along with a refill, and I dug in. Someone had left the Daily Mirror on the next table, so I snagged it and started reading.

A story on the front page detailed the escapades of one Sir Reginald Skelton, an industrial tycoon who had been rescued from the side of Annapurna in Nepal after his Sherpa fell and broke a leg.

Mention of the name Skelton reminded me that I needed to call Freddie, since we hadn't been able to hook up last time. This time, I caught him in the office and brought him up to date on our London adventure. Naturally, he was interested in joining the junket, especially when I related the fate of our agent.

"You need me over there, obviously," Freddie was saying.

"I don't think so, buddy."

"You can't handle it on your own, Beers."

"Hello? Lena is here with me. She's handling the research."

"That's not what I'm talking about. You need muscle. In case things get rough."

"Muscle? And you're the one supplying said muscle, I suppose."

"You need me to watch your back. Think about how many times you've gotten deep into something and got roughed up."

He had a point there. The last couple of incidents involving the store had resulted in minor bodily harm. I survived, but it made me skittish.

"You're just trying to finagle a trip to London," I accused. "Don't you have games to cover?"

"Bro, it's the slow season. Football's over. College basketball season is done. It's like the TV season after the Sweeps—not much happening."

"Freddie, thanks, but I don't need you. There's no chance of anything dangerous happening to me or Lena on this trip." These words would come back to haunt me. "Besides, we've almost got this wrapped up. We'll be heading back before you get to the airport."

"You know things always take longer than you think," he responded. "I need to get away. And you need me to keep you from going off on some wild goose chase."

This was some assertion coming from Freddie, who was solely responsible for the dearth of geese in the Twin Cities. I could have ticked off a half-dozen futile episodes he had led me on in the last year, including the wedding reception where we almost caused a rumble, but what was the point?

"Freddie, there's no way—"

"Listen here, Biersovich. You remember when I had to do that piece on the State Fair and they made me eat all that crap? Fried Snickers on a stick. Fried pork chop on a stick. Fried turkey leg on a stick—"

"Turkey leg on a stick? The leg *is* a stick. That doesn't make any sense."

"You're missing the point. I've paid my dues. I was sick for four days after eating all that junk. The assignment sucked, the food sucked, the story I wrote sucked..."

"Well, at least you admit it."

"I'm a sportswriter! I'm supposed to write sports! Not this feature shit!"

"And how is coming over here going to help you write sports?" I asked.

"I'm working on an angle."

"Say, Freddie, I was just reading this story about Sir Reginald Skelton. Any relation?"

"You laugh, but I think I do have an Uncle Reggie in Falmouth. Lives in a castle or something. I've never met him."

I was stunned. The story said this guy had been flown to his estate in Falmouth following the rescue. Could Freddie really be related to this mogul?

"I think this is the same guy, Freddie." I read him the story, and it seemed to make sense to him.

"My grandmother was born in Sheffield, divorced my grandfather, moved to America and remarried. My mom has two sisters and a brother. Meanwhile, my grandfather remarried and had three sons, one of them named Reggie. So I guess he's my half-uncle. Mom said she met him once when Grandpa Toodie brought them to England for a visit. She was about 14 or 15. Said Reggie was a 'ricker,' whatever that is."

"I would imagine he's changed in the last 40 years."

"Sounds like he's a rich playboy."

Foolhardy, I thought, just like his nephew. But I didn't say that out loud.

"I've never met your mother, Freddie. I think it's time I did."

"Forget about it."

"But you've met my Dad."

"Yeah, how is Pops? He still banging your boss?"

"Freddie, that's atrocious. Besides, she's not my boss anymore."

"Right. Sorry. I meant is he still banging your *girlfriend's* boss?"

"I gotta go."

"Hey, Beers, you ever wonder why they call it a U turn?"

"Not really, Freddie."

"Well, it's not really a U turn. It's more of an upside-down-U turn."

"You been smoking that funny weed again?"

"Why is that the first thing you ask me whenever we have a conversation?"

"Because no one in their right mind comes up with some of the bizarre ideas you have, Freddie. You're an original. An original lunatic, that is."

"You cut me, Beers."

"Could you get to the point? My meter's running."

"Beers, get me Sir Reggie's phone number. I'm going to give him a call. It's probably time I met him."

"Freddie, don't be ridiculous."

"I think maybe I need to come over there and visit him."

Interior groan number six thirty-nine. "No, you don't."

"I might be an earl. A lord. I might inherit a castle or something. I need to know about that."

"Freddie, you're not an earl, believe me. You're more likely related to Red Skelton than this guy."

"Then forget it. I'll find it on my own. Oh, by the way, you might want to give Tina a call."

"I tried to but she didn't have time to talk."

"Well, give me your number and I'll have her call you."

I wasn't about to give Freddie the number. "That's OK. I'll see her in a day or so."

10

There was little I could do but pass the time until Lena completed her tasks. I briefly thought about heading to the newspaper office to try to gain access to the archives, but I reckoned Lena would find out plenty enough information and more efficiently than I could.

When I have time on my hands, I usually work on my music collection, sorting and listening. With an ocean separating me from my passion, I did the next best thing—went in search of more musical treasures.

By this time, I knew my way down Portobello Road and returned to the scene of my previous excursions, the Mercy Beats shop. Jillian recognized me right away and remembered that I was a seeker of rare albums and tapes.

"Nuffin today in store, love, but I do 'ave somfin you may be keen to see," she said. She dangled a key in front of my face.

"What's that?"

"Key to me uncle's flat," she said. "'E said we could 'ave a look."

The excitement must have shown on my face because she said, "Calm down, Jim. I don't get off 'ere for another 'alf-hour." Just enough time for a quick one, so I popped down to the pub on the corner for a pint. Jillian was waiting on the sidewalk when I returned and pointed me toward an ancient yellow Vauxhall down the block. We motored through the back streets to an apartment block in Watford, where we climbed the steps to her uncle's flat.

As she unlocked the door, she admonished me. "We're 'ere just to look, not touch." The door opened to a living room that seemed like a treasure hunter's dream. Instead of chests of gold and jewels, however, piles of boxes full of records and tapes filled my vision.

"Me uncle worked for a top of the pops station thir'y years ago," Jillian explained, as I walked through the clutter. "This was back in the vinyl era. 'E was one of the well-known deejays, got all the big acts to come on his show.

"Sometimes 'e taped 'em, others not. 'E had a great tape of 'Endrix jamming when in walks Mick. Mick was scattin' over Jimi. Fantastic!"

"Wow. Is that tape here? I would love to hear it."

She looked around at the room. "Yeah, it's 'ere. Somewhere." She laughed.

Her uncle's collection left a lot to be desired in the organization department. Looking around, I estimated it would take a full week just to get things sorted properly. It would take several months to listen to everything.

A plan started formulating in my overworked brain. Maybe there was a way I could turn this into an archiving job. This was exactly the type of career I was looking for—something right up my alley of expertise.

The only trick was figuring out how to make it pay. That would take a little more study.

I suppose I could become a rock detective, concentrating on solving cases involving the murder of pop stars. There was a drawback to this notion. Few rock stars fell victim to murder; most opted out early in a more conventional manner—via drugs. The ones that didn't kill themselves early on using chemicals suffered the effects later in life in more mundane fatal diseases, such as cancer.

Besides, the only detecting I wanted to do was finding those rare musical gems at rummage sales and thrift shops.

"Let me run something by you, Jillian. I have my own collection of rock 'n' roll. It's a bit more organized than this," I said, indicating the jumble around us. She laughed. "I'm pretty good as an archivist, if I do say so myself. Do you think your uncle would be interested in hiring me to sort out this mess?"

She regarded me. "Hiring you? What, like a paying job?" She laughed again. "I don't think so."

"Consider this: He's probably got some rare stuff in these boxes, as you indicated. Probably some very valuable items. He could be sitting on a gold mine and not know it."

"Well, 'e don't care about that, love. Seems to get on well wif what 'e's got."

"Could you just run that by him? I could turn this collection into a showpiece, and he could make some serious coin. You know what rare discs go for in your shop."

She nodded.

"Well, just think about the potential of this hodgepodge of golden oldies. He wouldn't *have* to sell, but at least he would have a catalog of what he's got. In case he needed cash later." My arguments seemed to be swaying her.

"Well...I'll ask 'im, but I don't think 'e wants to do it if 'e 'asn't done it already. Probably won't want to pay for it in any event."

Without being able to handle the merchandise, there was little I could do. But before leaving, I counted four boxes full of forty-fives, seven boxes and bins of LPs and another six boxes of eight-tracks and cassettes. That didn't include the piles on various tables, chairs and the floor. I could see the spines of many a rare recording in the mishmash. It was a bloody mess and a bonanza at the same time.

Jillian dropped me back at the shop before heading home, and I continued my search. She was right—nothing worth acquiring today. I wandered down the street to check the other shops.

There was one I hadn't noticed on previous forays called Chukker Fun Shoppe. What caught my eye was a *Meet the Beatles* album in the window. The proprietor told me, however, that it was the cover only, no disc. I puttered around the store a bit, looking at the various novelties on sale—fake vomit, fuzzy dice, Mexican jumping beans, tape-on moustaches. Any gag gift you could imagine.

Then I spotted some exploding cigars, and a devious plan unfolded in my brainpan. One of these might be a great way to prank Freddie, the king of stinky smokes. I imagined his stunned expression when the trick blew up in his face, so I headed to the register with a wicked grin to buy it.

As it was getting on toward cocktail hour, I decided to head back to the hotel and try to hook up with Lena for dinner. She was way ahead of me, staked out at a table in the mostly full lobby lounge, sipping what looked like a Manhattan. A mountain of papers was on the table beside her drink.

"Where ya been, chief?"

"Investigating a musical nest egg. You found some more information, I see." I shed my jacket and put it on the back of a chair. "Order me a beer, will you? Have to hit the can."

When I returned from the restroom, I spotted Lena just as she was firing up a smoke with a match. That's weird, I thought. She doesn't smoke. As I approached, I saw it was a cigar. In a moment of panic, I checked the pockets of my jacket—empty.

"Lena, don't—"

I didn't get another word out before it exploded loudly, shocking Lena, me and everyone in near proximity. There was a bewildered expression on her face. Before I could explain, several men rushed over from nearby tables to see if she was OK.

"What I was trying to tell you...," I began, suppressing my instinct to laugh. She put the now-shredded cigar down, stood up, leaned over and whispered in my ear: "I'm goin' upstairs ta change my undahware." Then she left.

The other patrons wandered back to their tables. Then a man in a jacket bearing the hotel's insignia arrived at my table. In his wake was a burly Oriental with close-cropped hair, who looked like a refugee from a James Bond movie.

"Sir, are you a guest at this hotel?" the man asked.

"Yes, I'm in room—"

"Come with me, please," he said, backing up a step.

"But I have to wait—"

"This way." He indicated a path toward the front desk. I got up and proceeded as indicated.

Arriving at the front desk, he nodded at the man behind the counter, who invited me to settle my bill and collect my belongings. I didn't understand until he said I was no longer a guest and would have to find accommodations elsewhere.

No amount of explaining could sway them, and after a few minutes I gave up. Oddjob escorted me into the elevator and up to my room, overseeing my hasty packing job. He shook his head slowly when I inquired whether I could at least alert my traveling companion about what was transpiring.

On my way back down to the front desk, I remembered something that had gotten me out of a jam in a previous instance. It made no sense to me but it worked. So I thought why not give it a try.

The clerk was waiting for me to settle up, but I stood there staring at him for a moment. Then I said the magic phrase: "Buttered scones."

He gave me a funny look, then said, "Beg pardon?"

"Buttered scones."

"No, I'm afraid that's out of the question," he replied. "Our kitchen is closed to you." He gave me the hard-ass squint that said my eviction was irrevocable. Oh well. What happens in Vegas apparently doesn't happen in London.

I paid my bill with a large wad of pounds, then the presumed martial arts expert led me out to the sidewalk, where he spoke the only words I heard him utter: "Have a nice day." Then he went back inside.

And there I was on the sidewalk, with a rolling suitcase and a garment bag, considering my next move. I dialed the hotel and asked for Lena's room. She wasn't in, so I left a message and told her I would be at the pub. Since I didn't get to drink my beer at the lobby bar, I was still mighty thirsty. I ordered two pints, for starters.

11

You gotta be kiddin' me!" Lena was flabbergasted and still a little pissed about the trick cigar. I tried to explain that it was her own fault for going into my jacket behind my back. But that didn't fly.

And now I was out on the street and needed to find another hotel. I asked the waitress if there was a hotel in the immediate vicinity, other than the one I was evicted from. She thought a minute, then suggested a boutique hotel about three blocks away.

"Boutique? What is that, exactly?" I asked.

"Well, it's not your top-line hotel," she explained. "Fewer services. But it will do for the basics. Oh, the staff is Indian."

"Indian?"

"Or maybe Pakistani?" She frowned, shrugged and left to attend to another customer.

"So you gonna move ta dat place?" Lena asked.

"What choice do I have?"

"Dunno. Just thought Scalabrino had a little more clout than dat."

Yes, maybe I should let Joe T know what's going on, I thought. Maybe there's another hotel he knows of that would be on the preferred list.

"You got what?!" Joe T shouted when I relayed the news.

"It's a misunderstanding. See, Lena didn't know it was a trick cigar—"

"I cannot believe you're screwing around like this when you're supposed to be working! Do I need to tell Johnny about this?"

"No! Absolutely not! I can handle it. I just need to move to a new hotel. Should only be one more day anyway because the renovator will be there in the morning and we can wrap this up."

There was silence on the other end of the line. Joe T was thinking about something. Finally, he spoke. "Let me call you back. I have an idea."

"If you goin' ta da new place, I guess I need ta check out too," Lena said.

"Well, let's wait until I see what this boutique place looks like. It may be a rat hole."

"You wanna go check it out now?"

"No. Let's have another round. Maybe Joe T will call back with a suggestion."

"Awright, but no cigars."

Lena opted for bourbon this round. I assumed she was still a bit shaken by the prank. Disregard the fact that she had spoiled my surprise for Freddie. I'd have to come up with some other gag gift.

Joe T called back just as we were going to order a final round.

"Tell Lena to check out. I'll have a car sent to the front of the hotel in 30 minutes. Be ready."

"OK. Where are we going?"

"Just be ready." He hung up.

"Lena, pack your bags. We're both moving."

"Just as well," she replied. "I think a lady in da elevatah looked at me funny aftah I wet my pants."

I waited out on the sidewalk for Lena to come down. No sense antagonizing the staff any further. At the 40-minute mark, a black cab rolled up and the driver tooted.

"You Mr. Beers?" the elderly driver asked. He was wearing a gray vest and flat cap and looked like a stable hand.

"Yes. Just waiting on my companion." I held up a finger, then dialed the front desk to connect to Lena's room. The line started ringing as she walked out the door.

"Chilly out heah tonight," she said. The driver had opened the boot and stowed my luggage, then Lena's, and we climbed in.

"We need to go—" I began.

"I know where you're going, gov'nah," he said.

"Well, OK then," I said, exchanging a shrug with Lena.

But we didn't go a few blocks away to the "boutique" hotel. We went many blocks, perhaps a dozen. Then the cab stopped in front of an old brownstone on a very tidy street. I wasn't sure where we were.

"Here you are, gov'nah." The cabbie turned and pointed to the short flight of stairs leading up to the building.

"Is this the hotel? I don't see a sign," I said.

He just laughed.

"How much do I owe you?"

He laughed again, got out and unloaded our luggage onto the sidewalk.

"Have a nice evening, gov'nah. Ma'am," he said, tipping his cap.

"You sure we at da right place?" Lena asked as he drove off.

"No. Not at all," I said. A door opened at the top of the stairs and a woman in a short white dress, fitted to show off her curves, signaled to us.

"Are you Mr. Biersovich?"

"Yes, I am. Jim. And this is Lena."

"Welcome! Come on in," she said, stepping aside to let us enter. The dark, wood-paneled foyer led directly to a wide staircase, covered in ornate carpeting, leading to the second floor. Around both sides of the stairway were corridors, with a pair of doors on each side.

The woman, slightly shorter than Lena but every bit as gorgeous, led us up the stairs, and I summoned most of my willpower not to admire her silky legs. At the top of the flight, directly ahead, was a door marked "No. 3." She opened it and led us in.

"We'll start with the north wing first," she said in a classic British accent. "As you can see, we enter into the library. Very comfortable, lots of good reads in here. Oh, the fireplace is non-working so don't go mucking about with it. The piano is quite old and very out of tune. Then beyond, you see, through this doorway, you have a hall. Here's bedroom number one...the middle one is the office...then the bath...and your master off the bath."

I wanted to linger a bit longer in the bathroom because it was the most ornate one I had ever seen. Gold-framed mirror, speckled black granite countertops with three sinks, a walk-in towel closet, Jacuzzi, shower and tub. I could have lived there.

"Kitchen here," she continued, leading us into what looked like it could well serve a restaurant: three stoves, four sinks, two refrigerators, a chest freezer and a pantry the size of a small bedroom surrounding a built-in preparation table in the middle of the room. "There's quite a bit of leftover party food in the silver fridge over there, so help yourself."

As she led us back through the wing she explained, "We had a bit of a party here last night, but it's all shipshape now. The cleaning crew were in this morning and put in fresh linen, so you should be comfy.

"Now, through this corridor...there's your front door, of course...you enter the south wing. Game room in here...the felt on the table is new, by the way. Fireplace here does work but the flue sticks a bit, so mind that. Do you smoke, by any chance?"

Lena and I shook our heads.

"Good, well, if you must smoke, or have guests who do, this is the smoking room. We try to keep that contained. Bar on that side...should be fully stocked, so help yourself. Nice view of the street out these windows, as you can see. It's mostly quiet round here.

"Now down this hallway, bedroom...bedroom...loo...bedroom ...kitchen and laundry...back porch out here...also a smoking area, if needed." She concluded her spiel and looked at us. "Any questions?"

There were plenty of questions in my mind, but I didn't know where to start. Lena obviously didn't either. She had a stunned look on her face, like, "Is this place real?"

"Very well, then." The woman handed me a key and a card that had her name: Vi Capriola.

"Vi?"

"Short for Olivia. Those are my particulars. If you need anything, if the plumbing goes wonky," she giggled, "just call and I'll send someone round. Good evening." And then she was gone.

Lena and I exchanged a silent communication, then I said it out loud: "Did that really happen?"

"Not sure, chief, but I ain't complainin'," she said.

We gathered our luggage from the top of the staircase and selected our accommodations. Lena took a room in the north wing and I took the south. Naturally, she wanted the best bathroom. But the one on my side wasn't too shabby either.

I concluded I should have pulled that exploding cigar trick on the first day.

"Who was dat?" Lena asked after we reconvened in the north wing kitchen to forage for a late snack.

I pulled out the card. "Her name's Vi Capriola. I have no idea who that is. There's just a number and email address on the card."

"Why doncha ask Joe T?"

"Probably should thank him for rescuing us," I agreed. Of course, the call went to voicemail. I thanked him profusely for the new lodging and said I would call the next day when our mission was concluded.

After sampling the goodies on the party trays and taking another circuit around the living quarters, we went over our game plan.

Lena decided she was finished with research and only needed to acquire blueprints from the building inspector. I gave her £137 from our allowance to purchase them. She would do that while I met with the renovator. Then we could put a bow on our assignment and present it to the big boss.

Easier said than done.

12

Wednesday, April 11

After a restful, dream-free sleep, I awoke famished and headed to the south kitchen. Plenty of stuff with which to concoct breakfast, but I didn't feel like doing it. I took a chance that Lena had herself a bit more together on her wing.

There was coffee in her kitchen but no sign of the big breakfast buffet I was craving. Fixing a cup, I wandered down the hall and discovered Lena was already dressed and at work on a computer in the office.

"Thanks for the coffee," I called from the doorway.

"Found out where we are," she said. "Chelsea. Go dat way about a half-dozen blocks, you at da rivah."

"Where's the Tube station?"

"Ovah heah," she said, pointing at the map on screen. "Sloane Square."

"How did you figure this out?"

"Went down ta da cornah, looked at da street sign."

"So who lives here? Is it that Vi woman?"

"Ain't figured dat out yet."

"Well, it's pretty nice."

"Bettah dan your apawtment. Hell, bettah dan my condo," Lena said.

"Too bad we're about to leave town. This would be a nice place to hang for a while."

After scrounging for toast and jam, I cleaned up my act and prepared for what I surmised would be the final rendezvous. We hit the Tube, Lena going one way and me another.

At five minutes till 10, I rounded the corner to the front of the building. A man I hadn't seen before was standing there. He was wearing a dark suit sans tie, with a rosebud in the lapel.

"Hi, I'm Jim."

"Mr. Biersovich, ah yes." He extended his hand and I shook it. "Omar Tilden. I own the agency." He put on a grim face. "I'm afraid I have some bad news."

Not the sort of thing you want to hear first thing in the morning. I imagined that Charlene's condition had deteriorated or, worse yet, she had died of her injuries.

"Is it Charlene?" I asked.

"Oh, no. No, no. She'll be fine given a few more days. At least the doctors say she's out of danger. No, I'm afraid the bad news relates to the Fanshaw property." He turned slightly and nodded toward the front door.

"You mean this building?"

"Yes, quite so. It seems a member of the family has had second thoughts about divesting. I'm afraid we may not be able to move forward with the purchase agreement." He frowned. Just then, the renovator strolled up, with another man behind him, both in overalls.

"Morning," he said, extending his hand to Tilden. "Garry Naughton, I'm with Rejuvenesense. This is Ronnie Greene, the architect." Handshakes all around, then Tilden delivered the sad tidings. Naughton put his hands on his hips and muttered a "Fuck!" Greene, with a camera around his neck and carrying a kit bag, looked up and snapped a photo of the facade.

"What do you suggest we do now?" I asked Tilden.

"Well, the premises are off-limits to us for the moment. I'm attempting to get in touch with the family to sort this out. I suspect we may be put off for a bit." He bit his lower lip and regarded the three of us.

Naughton threw up his hands and shook his head. He was obviously pissed about this latest snag. "Two days in a row," he muttered. Greene seemed to take it in stride and shot a couple more pictures of the building before announcing, "Well, I'm off. Call me if it changes, Garry." Naughton shook his head and left also.

"Sorry about this," Tilden said. "We're as keen to finalize the deal as you are. Here's my card. If you haven't heard from me by tomorrow this time, please call."

Great. Another kink in the plan that likely was going to keep us here yet another day. On the bright side, we had much more comfortable housing. I decided it was cocktail and billiards hour and headed back to our new headquarters.

Lena was already there when I arrived, ensconced in a big, comfy-looking leather chair by a roaring fireplace. On the lamp table by her chair was a drink that I surmised was a screwdriver.

"Cocktail hour?" I asked.

"Just some OJ," she replied. "But you can twist my awm."

While I spiked her drink and splashed some out-of-my-normal-price-range scotch over ice for me, Lena said she got the blueprints and believed she had completed her research. I let her take a sip and nod approval before delivering the rebuttal.

"You gotta be kiddin' me!" she exclaimed.

"I wish I were. Tilden said he'd call if the situation changed."

"You bettah let Joe T know what's up."

"Good idea." It was still pretty early back home, but a glitch like this could put a big kink in the works.

Joe T was already awake when I called about 5:15 a.m. his time. Paring the report down to the essentials, I brought him up to speed and asked for his recommendation.

"Johnny isn't gonna like this," he said after a pause.

"Well, really not much we can do until they hear from the family."

"No, you can do something. You can go visit these people and get this straightened out today."

That didn't sound like something I wanted to do or was even qualified for. "I don't think that's the proper channel—"

"Screw the channel! Let's cut out the middle man and go to the source. Who's the family?"

"Tilden said the name was Fanshaw."

"Fanshaw? Never heard that one. I'll call Vi and see if she can find out who they are."

"Speaking of Vi, thanks again for putting us in this fabulous home. Is Vi on Johnny's staff?"

Joe T chuckled. "You could say that. Probably quite a bit while he was in London recently." He laughed some more and said he'd call back later.

"What's da buzz?"

"He said we need to go visit the family and try to convince them to sell."

"Wayah dey live?"

"Dunno. He's gonna call Vi and have her find out."

"Da lady what let us in heah?"

"Yeah. Strange…he sounded weird when I asked if she was on the Scalabrino team."

"Dey's prolly a story dere."

"Look through your research and see if you see the Fanshaws mentioned. I'm going to get some lunch and make a couple more calls."

"Gotcha. I could use a snack myself."

We delved deeper into the fridges and found even more party food: all sorts of cheeses, trays of sliced meat, a fruit medley, veggies and dip. It seemed a shame to let it go to waste, so we did our part.

Emmie was first on my list when I started dialing.

"Sorry for calling so early but things have been very strange," I began.

"That's OK. You have it all wrapped up?"

"No, that's the problem. There's a snafu that we've got to try to fix. The owners are balking at selling."

"That's too bad. So you think you'll be there another couple days?"

"Possibly."

"Tina came by the store yesterday. We had a nice visit. I don't think she's real happy right now. She said she wished you'd call."

"I did call her, but she didn't have time to talk. I'll try again, though."

We chit-chatted a bit more, then concluded our call when Lena came into the kitchen to report her findings.

"No Fanshaws," she said. "Current ownah listed as FFT Limited. Just a post awfiss box."

"OK, I guess it's up to Joe T and Vi then."

"You mind if I go shoppin' a bit?" Lena asked. "Don't know when I'll evah get back heah."

"May as well. But call me in case they locate these folks. I wouldn't want you to run out of money before we wrap this up."

13

Lena promised to check in hourly and headed down to the Tube station. I rang Tina's number and finally made the connection.

"Hey, Beers, good to hear from you."

"Emmie says she saw you at the store yesterday."

"Just visiting." She hesitated. "Actually, I came by to see what I could find out at cosmetics."

"You investigating the robbery?"

"No. That's just it. They won't let me look into it, even though I know all the clerks and can probably get them to tell me vital information."

"I don't understand."

"Idiots are too stupid to see I could help with this case. They've got me riding playground patrols and said if I complain they'll put me on meter violations."

"But you came by the store to investigate...?"

"On my lunch hour. Somebody ratted me out to the sergeant. Now he's on my ass to 'just do my job,' as he puts it, and leave the investigating to the detectives."

Tina sounded really frustrated with her predicament, and I didn't know how to help her. "I'm sorry you're in this situation. Is there any chance—"

"Beers, I'm staring down years of menial assignments, 'paying my dues,' they call it, with not much prospect of advancement. This isn't what I signed on for."

"Well...what are you gonna do?"

"I don't know. I'm thinking...this sounds crazy, I know...maybe I should go back to the store. They have an opening in cosmetics."

My heart leapt for joy. This was an exciting development—the team back together again. I didn't want to sound too eager to have her chuck her dream career, but I missed seeing her every day as I entered La Scala.

"An opening?"

"Melissa, the woman who was pistol-whipped? She's on medical leave and has already indicated she's not coming back."

"Pistol-whipped? First I've heard of this."

"They brought in a guy from Vegas—"

"Roger Thompson."

"Yeah. I chatted with him a bit, and he seems pretty clueless."

"As I expected."

"Bambi is helping him out." She laughed. "Can you imagine?" Bambi Schroeder is one of the store's fashion buyers and apparently expendable since she had previously served as elf assistant during my short-term stint as Santa. Then Tina lowered her voice and said wistfully, "We made a pretty good team, didn't we?"

It choked me up a bit. "We still can," I responded.

"Look, I gotta go. I've got your number, so I'll try to keep you up to date on what's going on here."

I told her good times to call, then I rang Jane Mertin and dropped a not-so-subtle hint that the store could really use Tina's expertise in my absence. As head of facilities, Jane's purview included shoplifting and other crimes against La Scala. I intimated that Tina should be encouraged to return to her post at La Scala with some sort of financial incentive. Jane seemed receptive to the idea.

While I was passing the time knocking around pool balls, Joe T called with the address. The Fanshaws had an estate in Luton and would have a driver meet us at noon at the Luton airport. When Lena checked in, she sounded disappointed that she had to curtail her retail quest.

It was a 45-minute bus ride to the Luton airport north of London, where an ancient Bentley picked us up at the designated spot. The driver was in a gray Nehru jacket and told us with a sneer that his name was Marston, but he didn't say whether that was his first or last name.

We sat in the back, where Lena leaned over and whispered, "Sump'n creepy 'bout dis guy." I shrugged it off. After all, we were in a foreign country for the first time, and had a lot to learn about their ways. The only other person I had encountered who had a driver was Johnny Scalabrino, and some might consider him creepy also.

Marston was mute as he took us out of the city proper, across a rolling countryside to a long, heavily treed drive up a hill, then down through what I imagine they call a "copse" over there, emerging into a clearing that revealed an expansive country manor. It was three stories and about a block long. Marston pulled up the circular drive to the front steps.

We expected him to open the back door for us, but he didn't budge. After an awkward pause, Lena and I exchanged a look, then bailed out of our respective sides of the back seat. The not-so-personable Marston simply jerked his thumb over his shoulder, indicating the door, then pulled away in the Bentley.

"Creep," Lena muttered, as we watched him depart.

"I suppose you've been introduced to Marston." The voice behind us at the top of the stairs startled us. It was a tall chap, elderly, wearing what looked like fox-hunting gear.

"Hi, I'm Jim. This is Lena."

"Yes, I surmised as much. Please come in." He led the way through a dark hallway filled with portraits and doors off to either side. At the end, we entered a kitchen, where another elderly man and a woman sat at a table. He indicated the empty chairs and asked if we would like some tea.

The kitchen was large, with a butcher block table in the center on which lay a meat cleaver. Along one wood-paneled wall, pots and pans of varying sizes were hung, with a window in the center over the sink. The opposite wall held pantry shelves filled with copious amounts of canned goods, flour, assorted pasta in tall jars and loaves of odd-shaped bread. And at the near end, in an alcove under a picture window, was the dining table where we sat.

After introductions all around, we learned that the people in attendance were siblings. The man who met us at the top of the stairs was John Fanshaw and at the table was his brother James. Serving tea was their sister, Helen Lester.

"I suppose you're here to discuss the property," John began.

"Yes, sir. My employer, Mr. Johnny Scalabrino of Minneapolis, is very interested in acquiring that site."

"Yes, quite so. Well, I'm afraid we've got some persuading to do."

"How so?" I asked.

John got up and went to the counter adjacent to the sink, where he retrieved a folder, then sat back down. He removed a sheet of paper from the folder, stared at it a few seconds, then turned it and placed it so Lena and I could peruse it.

"The property is held in the name of the trust. As you can see, Bitsy, Jimmy and I are listed as beneficiaries, along with our half-brother, Stony."

Halfway down the page was a list of names under FFT Limited: John Jasper Featherstonaugh, Helen Marie Featherstonaugh Leicester, James Ronald Featherstonaugh, Samuel Keith Perkins and Jasmine Sloane.

"Feather-stone-aw?" Lena asked.

"Who is Helen Lie-chester?" I asked.

"Pronounced 'Fanshaw,' and 'Lester,' " James said. "Helen is Bitsy. Featherstonaugh Family Trust have been managing that property, along with several others, including this estate, since the passing of our dear mum some years ago."

"Who are Samuel Perkins and Jasmine Sloane?" I asked.

Helen and John looked at each other, then Helen muttered, "Slut."

"Now, Bitsy. Ms. Sloane is the common-law wife of Stony—Samuel Perkins. We suspect she is the fly in the ointment, as it were."

"I don't understand. She's not a sibling but...what? She can veto decisions of the group?"

"Let me explain. Stony is somewhat younger, you see. Mum treated him as her favorite when she remarried, sort of like a puppy. He had her ear toward her final days and persuaded her to amend the trust to include...that woman."

"Trollop," Helen muttered.

"He don't wanna sell?" Lena asked.

James smirked. "Your accent is delightful."

"Yours ain't so bad yaself," she replied.

"No," John said, "it's not that he doesn't want to sell. It's...rather complicated, I'm afraid."

"So can we talk to him?" I asked. "Mr. Scalabrino wants property in that area, and since your building is unused—"

"That's exactly what we've been trying to do—talk to him. He's buggered off somewhere and scuppered the program."

Lena and I stared with question marks on our faces.

"He's gone missing. We can't sell till we find him and get him to agree," John translated. "Provisions of the trust."

"I see. Does he live here?"

Bitsy laughed. "I should say not!"

"He's got a place up the road a couple of miles," James explained. "That woman said he went off without leaving a note. Been gone for two days."

"Maybe he's just on a business trip?" I offered.

"Hah!" Bitsy interjected. "More like staying one step ahead of the bobbies."

"Stony has had some...dodgy dealings, you see," John explained. "And Jasmine..."

Bitsy mumbled something that sounded like bitch or witch. John didn't finish his thought.

This was a messy development, and we weren't equipped to deal with it. I excused myself, headed into the foyer and dialed Joe T. After a brief explanation of the problem, he cursed and said he would call back after discussing the situation with the boss.

Meanwhile, there was little we could do. The Featherstonaughs offered to show us around the estate, and before I could decline, Lena blurted that she'd love to see it. Oh well, I thought. That will give Joe T time to find a solution. Perhaps Scalabrino would make the family an offer it couldn't refuse.

14

Bitsy led the tour through the expansive lower level, with east and west wings, featuring a tremendous library, smoking room, huge kitchen, a laundry area as big as the library, an indoor pool and, just beyond the windows, a cricket pitch. A grand staircase, winding back on itself, led up to the second level, which opened onto a game room with two snooker tables, darts and a long bar. On either end were four large bedrooms, a couple of them closed off, and no less than four bathrooms.

The third floor held only an art studio, a study and a sewing room, with the rest of the space used for storage. We peeked briefly into the storage area, which was stuffed with crates, statuary and miscellaneous toys and knickknacks. It looked like a good place to conceal a body, but I certainly didn't want to go looking for one.

At the back of the house was a terrace that overlooked a garden, somewhat overgrown and in need of a caretaker. Bitsy explained that the longtime gardener had died recently in his 70s, and they hadn't gotten around to finding a replacement.

Beyond the garden was a field sloping up to woods. John said the estate extended into the next shire at one point, but their father had sold off land to buy properties in London, one of which was the warehouse.

"So getting back to your brother—hold on, I've got to take this call." I moved off the terrace and answered it. It was Joe T.

"Are you able to locate this fellow?"

"I'm not sure how. What do you suggest?"

"If you're thinking of contacting the police, you already know the answer. I'm sending Vi back to where you're staying. She has resources. If she can't help you locate the guy, no one can."

"OK, but—"

"Send in your report. I'll get Johnny to look it over and make sure this is the property he wants. Also, go back and check the other site again. Maybe we'll have to make a go of that if they won't sell this one. Get the renovator to give you an estimate on that one."

"But I thought—"

"When you leave there today, go check out where the guy lives. Talk to the wife. But don't let the siblings know you're doing it."

"I don't see how—"

"You running short of cash? We can get you some more. Just tell Vi what you need."

When Joe T gets on a roll like this, there's no talking my way out of it, if I know what's good for me. "OK. Will do."

Rats. Stuck on this assignment another day. Maybe two. This was turning out to be not such a quick-and-easy operation.

Rejoining the group, I thanked them for their hospitality but said we had to get going. I left them a card with my number and a request to call as soon as they heard from their brother, day or night.

The unsettling Marston drove us back to the Luton airport, where we checked the local directory and caught a cab to a pub in the heart of the city. Lena chatted up the bartender, a woman with blond hair in her 50s, and soon had the location of Stony Perkins' cottage. It was more than a stone's throw from the estate, more like all the way across the county.

The cabbie looked at us askance when we gave him the address, but he drove us there and reluctantly agreed to wait while we approached the door. It was a squat red brick house with a deteriorating roof behind a mostly brown lawn peppered with yard gnomes. Blue gazing balls flanked the door, which had a small window near the top.

"Who is it?" we heard a woman's voice call from behind the closed door.

"We're looking for Mr. Perkins. Stony."

"Who's we?"

"My name is Jim Biersovich and I'm with Lena Fangeaux. We're from America."

The door opened a crack and an eye peeked at us before opening farther. A woman possibly in her 30s, somewhat disheveled, looked us over. She had uncombed tawny hair that looked like it just arose from a nap. She was wearing an off-white, somewhat dirty sweatshirt over jeans with holes in the knees, no shoes.

"What do you blokes from America want with Stony?" she asked suspiciously.

"We were just speaking with his siblings—"

"Nasty buggers! If you're with them bleeding—"

"We're just here to try to buy some property that they own. They indicated that Stony is missing."

"We just tryin' ta find out why he don't wanna sell da propahty," Lena added.

"Are you Miss Sloane?" I asked.

The woman thought about it a few seconds, looked from me to Lena and back, then said, "I'm Jasmine Sloane. Why don't you come in and explain this."

She offered tea and we accepted, landing on a sofa in the living room covered with a green throw. While she put the water on, we examined the room. In the wall ahead was a small fireplace, unlit but full of charred wood and ashes. On either side of the fireplace were small suits of armor, child-size. Above the plain wooden mantle was a hunting scene—riders mounted and ready to set out on a fox hunt.

Scattered around the room were a number of black-and-white framed photos of children, possibly the siblings, engaged in play at the beach, bike riding and apple picking, mementos of happier times. In contrast to the estate we had just visited, the current dwelling was extremely modest. There were also some old photos of what looked like a warehouse and a bank. An upright piano stood in the corner.

When tea was served, Jasmine sat on a worn velvet armchair perpendicular to the sofa.

"You've got my attention," she said, sipping the tea. "Where's Stony?"

"That's what we came to ask you. His siblings said—"

I didn't get any further before she teared up and started crying. Lena stooped down beside her chair and held her hand. "It's OK," she said. "Tell us about it."

Between sobs she managed to give us the picture. James Featherstonaugh came over earlier in the week, perhaps Monday, to get Stony's signature on the proxy for sale. Stony said he had to run it by his solicitor and put him off. James indicated the timing was tight, and they didn't want to get put off "like last time."

"Last time?" I asked.

"I don't know what that meant, and Stony didn't explain. Anyway, he called up Beany—our solicitor—and they arranged a meet."

"Beany?" Lena asked.

"Beaton Dobbs. He was the attorney for the trust until the old man died. Then Stony's brothers decided to ditch him and hire another."

"What is Stony's relationship with his brothers?" I asked.

She scoffed. "He's the black sheep, ain't he? He's their half-brother, but it seems they would rather he just go away." She teared up again. "I guess they got their wish," she said between snuffles.

"When did you last see him?"

"He went off to pub Monday just after lunch."

"To meet with the lawyer?" I asked.

She shrugged.

"Did you call the police?"

She sneered at that. "What bleeding for? They wouldn't lift a bloody finger to find him. That lot at the estate have poisoned his name."

Jasmine gave us the name of the pub and the address of the attorney. Once again, we were being called on to do the work of the police, investigating what potentially could be a crime, perhaps kidnapping—at the very least a missing persons incident.

THE BARTENDER at the Luton Rathskeller conceded that old Stony was a character and visited the pub infrequently, but they hadn't seen him this week, certainly not on Monday.

About a mile away was the office of Beaton Dobbs, who looked like a character out of Dickens: elderly, short, rotund, watch chain in his vest, balding, muttonchop whiskers.

"Call me Beany," he said, as we sat across from him in his office. "Stony has gone missing, eh? That's troubling. Have the police been notified? No? Well, not surprised. Yes, Stony said something about meeting me Monday afternoon to look over a contract." He consulted the calendar on his desk. "I was in court till about 2:30, so we had arranged to meet at 3. But he never showed. Not unusual for Stony, though. He can be sort of a...loose gun. When old Stony gets a notion, well...he may have just gone off on one of his larks."

"Where do you think he's gone?"

He hesitated before answering. "He can be one for the ladies."

"A girlfriend?"

"He's been known to put it about. Did you inquire down at pub?"

"We just came from there."

"I see. He's quite infatuated with Jasmine."

"But you think he cheats on her."

"I don't know."

"Can you think of anyone who would want to do him harm?"

"Which agency did you say you were with?"

"La Scala. It's a department store in America. We're interested in purchasing the warehouse building on Knightsbridge. My employer has authorized us—"

His expression suddenly darkened. "Hmmm...that is a sticky situation. And you need Stony to finalize the deal, I suppose. Well, we'll just have to find him," he said with a smile. "I'll make inquiries." He stood and that was our signal that the meeting was ended.

"Let's revisit dat pub," Lena asked as we exited his office.

"You think you can get someone to tell us where Stony is?"

"Naw. I need a drink."

15

On the ride back into London, I had no less than four calls. Emmie dialed just to check up on me. I put on a brave face but told her there were complications that were likely to keep us apart a few more days. She whispered sweet nothings in my ear that increased my level of heartsickness.

Freddie called, surprising me, since I hadn't given him the number. But I suspected he weaseled it out of Tina. He reported that he had gotten a few days off and was on his way to the airport after speaking with his uncle, Sir Reggie, who was keen on American football and one of the investors in the recently folded London team. Sir Reggie was quietly campaigning to bring a franchise back to the city, and Freddie had somehow finagled doing a story on it.

"So I'll see you when I land, buddy," he said.

"Freddie, how the hell did you swindle this junket out of your editor?"

"It's not a junket. I'll be working, Beers. Doing stories. I'm also looking up a couple of ex-Vikings who are trying to catch on with the Scottish Claymores."

"Working. Good. So you won't have time to bother me."

"That's deeply hurtful, Beers. You think all I do is bother you?"

"I didn't say that, but I'm working here too, y'know. Besides, we'll probably be on our way back before you even get here."

"I'll see you in the morning," he said and clicked off.

Tina phoned and said the detective assigned to the La Scala case was incompetent and a womanizer to boot. He spent most of his time trying to pick up the women he interrogated and very little actually investigating. Also, Roger Thompson had no clue how the store operated; he thought it was just like Vegas. She said she was really thinking hard about chucking the law enforcement game and going back to the store after speaking with Jane Mertin. I did a little leap for joy internally.

"Say, have you spoken to Freddie recently?" I asked, trying to ascertain whether Tina was the source of the leaked phone number.

"No, why?"

"Uh, no reason. Keep me posted on what develops there."

Then Vi Capriola called and said she was waiting for us at the apartment with some information.

Lena asked to use the phone and made a mysterious call to someone named Raleigh, whom she informed she would be a couple more days in London. She was not forthcoming with details about who that was. Secret lover? I would definitely have to get Tina on the case.

Vi was indeed waiting for us on our return late in the afternoon. In the game room over a cocktail, she told us she had spoken with Joe T and was on the trail of the missing brother. Meanwhile, we were to contact the property agent and the renovator to set up a meet at 11 a.m. John Featherstonaugh was driving down to London to go through the building with us.

Also, to head off the possibility that this was a ploy to drive up the price, we were to spend the afternoon looking at the first apartment we had toured, plus a new site in the South Bank area across the Thames. Send in a report and after that we were free to make arrangements to return home, she added.

Yes! The news I had been waiting to hear. Not that London was an awful place, but I was missing Emmie terribly. For the first time I could recall, I felt like I was lacking a part of me, and I couldn't wait to get back to see her again.

"What exactly is your role in...all this?" I asked.

"I'm here to help you, Mr. Biersovich," Vi said.

"Yes, but what I mean is—"

"Where are you camped out?" she asked.

"Beers on dat side and I'm ovah heah," Lena said.

"Right, well, I'll join you on the north wing then," Vi said. "You have enough food left?"

"Plenty," I said.

"Good, well, I'll see you a bit later," she said, then left via the front door.

"You think Tina gonna come back ta da stoah?" Lena asked as we refreshed our drinks.

"Sure sounds like it. I hope that happens. She doesn't seem to be happy doing what she's doing."

"Yeah, I get dat impression."

"Lena, back there in the cab...who is Raleigh?"

She gave me a Mona Lisa smile. "I gotta go do some research, see can I find dis Stony," she said. "What you got goin'?"

"Nothing. You want to go somewhere this evening?"

"Naw. I'm just gonna rest up. Sounds like tamorrah gonna be busy." She left for the office down the hall.

I weighed my options. Hang out at the apartment and rest up, kick back and get blotto on the free booze or go out in search of adventure. Checking the clock, I saw that it was almost time for Jillian to get off, so I gave her a call.

"Funny you should call," she said. "I was just about to ring you."

"What's going on? You have something new for me?"

"Yeah," she laughed. "I should say. Me uncle says you can poke around 'is collection."

"Terrific!"

"Says 'e'll be there this evening. Want to go?"

"Sure! What time?"

"I'm about to leave 'ere...you remember the address?"

"I've got it written down. See you shortly."

Yes! Another piece of good news. I was on a roll. Lena was already in computer concentration mode when I informed her I was going out for a bit, and she barely nodded comprehension of my departure.

On the Tube ride over, I mentally catalogued my collection, noting the gaps I wanted to fill. There weren't many, seeing as I had been at it for years and had amassed what I considered a pretty impressive set of rock discs and tapes. But there were a few gems that would top off the compilation nicely—*if* Jillian's uncle had them and *if* I could persuade him to part with them.

When he answered the door, he wasn't anything like I had pictured him—a sort of disheveled Joe Cocker type in ratty jeans and a tie-dyed shirt, with a raging mop of wild hair. This was a slender fellow, shorter than me, in a three-piece suit, balding, wearing spectacles, rings on four fingers. He didn't go with the chaotic apartment.

"Lawrence Hickey," he said, shaking my hand. "Friends call me Hick."

"Very nice to meet you, sir. Jillian gave me a peek at your collection and I must say—"

"Quite a shambles, isn't it?" he asked with a laugh.

"Drink?" Jillian asked, heading for the kitchen.

"Whatever you're having."

"So Jilly says you're somewhat of a collector yourself," he said, clearing the sofa so we could sit.

"I have a few things of my own. Not nearly this much. Or rather..."

"Not nearly this messy?" he chortled.

"Well...you could use a bit of straightening up. I pride myself on the orderliness of my acquisitions."

"And you think you could turn this..." He waved his arm to indicate the rest of the room. "...into some sort of...I don't know...museum?"

"I just think you've got some valuable stuff here, potentially. But you can't tell what you have because it's all piled up, in boxes, scattered around..."

"What do you propose?"

I explained how my collection was set up, with floor-to-ceiling shelves, arranged alphabetically according to genre. He seemed to like that idea and indicated he knew where he could get some shelves rather quickly.

"In the meantime, I'd like to go through the boxes and sort things, put them in some kind of order, so that when you get your shelves, you'll be ready to display them."

He smiled. "And your fee for all this?"

"Well, sir..."

"Hick."

"Hick...I really wouldn't charge you anything. I mean..."

"Perhaps a selection from the collection as payment?"

Here was the suggestion I was hoping for, and he made it. "That would be excellent, Hick." We shook hands, and the deal was sealed. "I guess you'd better get to work then. I'll leave you to it." He departed, and Jillian smiled at me. "Good show. Any way I can 'elp?"

I explained how I wanted to attack the stockpile of discs methodically, one box or bin at a time. Jillian fetched some printer paper and I made signs that I spread around the floor for the different genres: acid rock, soul, blues, pop and so on. She grasped my scheme and attacked a box.

The hours flew by. We finished off a bottle of merlot and then most of a six-pack of beer. Empty boxes accumulated in a corner while piles of sorted discs grew. Among the collection I found a copy of *Yesterday and Today* with the butcher shop cover, the gift Emmie had given me at Christmas. When I thought we were nearing the end, Jillian began hauling more crates out of closets and a bedroom.

"You'll 'ave to 'elp me with the barrel," she said.

"Barrel?"

There was indeed a barrel, filled to the brim with sleeveless 45s, sitting in a corner of a bedroom. Calculating the number of discs within, I figured this alone was a full-day project and would have to wait.

Sorting was complicated by the fact that many of the tapes and cassettes were demos, marked only with a random number or date. No way to tell what they were without listening.

Jillian had pizza delivered at some point and I vaguely remember consuming a slice, but other than that, my sole focus was on searching and sorting. At the end, near midnight, the stacks of categorized music were impressive.

And there was one small stack of very special items that I had put aside. These were the rarities, the never-before-seen recordings—at least not by me. They included a gold master of *Flash Harry*, Nilsson's final studio album, not released in America; a demo tape labeled "Jagger + Morrison"; and a tape of a rare appearance of Aretha Franklin and Petula Clark on the same stage.

I left Jillian with the understanding that she would intercede with her uncle again, to take a crack at the barrel and to have my reward selected from the special cache I had put aside. As I rode the Tube back to No. 3, I was exhausted, nodding off, and my head was swimming with golden oldies, but one Petula Clark song in particular: "Don't Sleep in the Subway."

16

Thursday, April 12

G et yaself up, Beers." Lena was shaking me awake at what I thought was the middle of the night, but a glance at the bedside clock told me it was 9:45.

Throwing on a black sweatshirt and jeans, I hustled to the kitchen and came upon Lena conversing with Vi.

"Good, you're up," Vi said. "Now you can't miss your appointment. It's important. I'll be back this evening with, I hope, the location of our missing Mr. Perkins. Meanwhile, I trust you will get the rest of Mr. Scalabrino's task accomplished forthwith." She turned and left.

"Coffee," I croaked to Lena.

"Ya had a late night, eh, Beers?"

"Mmm."

"Little too much hooch?" she asked.

"That and information overload." I briefly described my evening and hopes that I would get another crack at it and be able to claim a nice reward.

"Ya got an hour ta pull yaself tagethah," Lena said. "I'll meet ya at da place. Gotta run anothah errand." Then she left also.

After a second cup, I was mostly awake, grazed on fresh crullers that had magically appeared and hit the shower. There were two messages on my phone—one from Tina saying she had discovered an important bit of information, and one from Jasmine Sloane, saying she remembered that Stony said he was going to have a quick one with his pal Davey before meeting with the lawyer. Did that sound important?

I rang her back and said yes, it sounded important. Who was Davey? High school chum, David Enthoven, ran a landscaping business. Stony would help him out on occasion. She said she called the business, but Davey claimed Stony never showed up. I got the address from her and promised to follow up on it.

At the appointed hour, I was standing in front of the store with Omar Tilden, Garry Naughton and Ronnie Greene. Tilden said we couldn't go in just yet as we were waiting for someone. That someone turned out to be John Featherstonaugh, who stepped out of his Bentley and nodded at the group. Then Tilden unlocked the door and we entered.

Both Naughton and Greene spent quite a bit of time measuring and sketching, while Featherstonaugh related the history of the building as he knew it. His father had purchased the vacant building in the 1930s. It was fairly run down and in need of major renovation, which was completed in 1938, when John was 5 years old.

It was leased as warehouse space for an import-export business supplying the burgeoning department stores of the district. During the war, however, there was less need for storing consumer goods and more demand for munitions storage, which his father accommodated until his untimely death in 1944. His wife, Abigail, assumed control of the property and soon remarried.

After the war, businesses were gearing back up and needed room to store supplies of office equipment such as desks, chairs and tables. Upper floors held boxed items, including stationery, hardware and dry goods. At one point, it was hosting storage for both Harvey Nichols and Harrods. That seemed ironic in light of my assigned task.

When the renovator and architect were finished with their examination, the group marched up to the second floor. This level took almost no time to survey, seeing as there were only a few offices. I refrained from entering the office where the body of the hobo had been found. Featherstonaugh had barely gotten into description of the Morgan auto dealership that took over the main floor in 1962 when the surveyors announced they were going up again.

Exiting into the hallway on the third level, Naughton and Greene headed toward the front of the building and started in those offices. The division of the third floor gave Featherstonaugh plenty of time to bring us up to date on the history of the building as far as his family's ownership was concerned.

I asked why the reversion to warehouse space and why that was eventually abandoned. He explained the revitalization of the downtown area, the City of London, pulled much of the office and warehouse space into that area, leaving them with few clients.

The tour moved down to the end of the floor, and the surveyors entered an office while we waited in the hall. Tilden was remarking on the lack of comparable space on Knightsbridge when we heard an "Oh my God!" from the room. When we entered, we saw Naughton and Greene standing on either side of a man lying on the floor with a pool of blood surrounding his head. It was déjà vu all over again, and goosebumps ran up my neck.

The back wall was ripped up and a pry bar lay on the floor next to the man.

"What happened?" Tilden asked.

"We came in here, saw this man on the floor," Greene said.

"Is he...?"

"I think he's dead," Naughton said.

We approached and after a few seconds, Featherstonaugh said, "My God! It's Stony!"

Tilden dialed the police, then warned us not to touch anything while we waited for them to arrive.

Featherstonaugh went into the hallway and we followed. He looked pale and loosened his tie as he leaned against the wall. We urged him to sit because it might be a while. He sat on the floor and put both hands on his face, muttering, "Stony, Stony, Stony."

Naughton didn't know what to do. They had measured and sketched half the building and wanted to complete the job. But Tilden advised against it, asking them to remain in place.

In time, Detective Constable S.J. Huntington arrived with a pair of bobbies and a team of emergency medical technicians, who pronounced the man dead at the scene. Huntington asked us to return to ground level and wait for him.

After 20 minutes, the EMT personnel left with a body bag, then Huntington came down and started questioning the group: names, addresses, who found the body, why were we in the building, who was the victim, why was he in the building, did we recognize the murder weapon, and so on.

Featherstonaugh explained that he was one of the owners, that his half-brother had recently gone missing and had been reluctant to sign a purchase agreement. He speculated that he was tearing the place up to make it less attractive to a buyer, perhaps to spite his siblings.

"Did you hear any noise when you entered the building?" Huntington asked.

We all shook our heads.

"And the front door was locked?"

"I unlocked it," Tilden said.

"Thank you, gentlemen. That's all for now. Here's my card." He handed one to each of us. "Please phone me if you think of anything else. This building will be sealed off until we've gone over it properly."

"But we're right in the middle of an inspection," Naughton said.

"I'm afraid you'll have to postpone it." He ushered us out the front door, got the key from Tilden, locked up and waited until his minions had sealed the front with crime tape.

Huntington took me aside and asked if I was the same gentleman who had been at the site when the previous body was found. I admitted I was. He asked if I knew a Thomas Waters. I said I was just visiting London and had only been in town a few days. He said in light of the new discovery, they would be looking at the Waters case as a potential homicide. Before he left, he advised me to be available for further interviews.

Naughton was beside himself. "I can't complete this job if it keeps being interrupted!" Greene shrugged, like no big deal. I suggested we head to the other site and try to get that survey completed, at the very least.

John Featherstonaugh looked dazed. Tilden asked if he could drop him somewhere, but he said his driver was coming, so Tilden brought his car around and the rest of us rode down to the apartment building.

Lena called on the ride and said she was sorry, couldn't make it to the building. I told her just as well, we had a little problem. She was stunned when I told her we discovered another dead body, and that body was none other than the missing brother. I told her there was no point in her showing up at the apartment building and that we should just meet up afterward. She said great, she was still running her errand.

"Be on the lookout for bodies," Greene joked as we entered. Tilden wasn't amused.

As we made the circuit of the first level of flats, Naughton asked, "You want this whole building sketched out? Because it's going to take quite a while and I can tell you from looking at it, if the other floors are like this, renovation will be expensive. I mean prohibitively expensive."

"No need to sketch everything. Most of the floors are like this one. And I just need something for comparison as far as renovation figures," I said.

We made it through the building without happening across any more cadavers, thank God, and Naughton reiterated his belief that turning the place into a department store would take a hefty investment. He promised to get a ballpark estimate on teardown to me in three days.

Greene said architecturally, there was nothing distinctive about the structure. It was like a blank canvas and would in some respects be easier to design.

Joe T called to see how it was going, and I filled him in on the latest snafu. When he asked if the second building was still a possibility, I related the comments of the renovator. He thought Scalabrino still preferred the warehouse building and asked for any updates I could give him, any time of day or night. Fortunately, we didn't need to look at the South Bank site because Scalabrino decided it was too far off the beaten path.

Meanwhile, I was to remain on the clock and on location. My triumphant return to my honey was looking like it would never happen.

17

When we finally finished the tour of the building and parted ways, I pulled out Huntington's card and gave him a call. For some reason, I decided to keep this information from the rest of the group.

"DC Huntington."

"Detective, this is Jim Biersovich, from the building site where we found the body—"

"Mr. Perkins."

"Yes. And I just wanted to call you because I remembered something that could be important." I was reading my notes to make sure I had it correct, naturally.

"Yes. Go on."

"I spoke with Mr. Perkins' wife yesterday, Jasmine. We were trying to locate him—"

"We?"

"My co-worker Lena Fangeaux. She's here helping me research the building."

"I see."

"And Jasmine said she thought Mr. Perkins was going to meet with a friend who's a landscaper. Name of David Enthoven. She thought he was the last person that might have seen him before..."

"David Enthoven. And where would this gentleman be located?"

"Up in Luton, I suppose. Where Mr. Perkins lives...lived."

"Thank you. We'll follow up with him. Anything else?"

"No. Just that for some reason Mr. Perkins was balking on signing a purchase agreement on the building. That's why we're here, Lena and me."

"I see."

"He was also supposed to meet with his attorney about it the day he went missing. Beaton Dobbs. Also in Luton."

"Very good. May I ask where was your associate this morning?"

"Lena? Well, she was out...running an errand."

"I'd like her to come in to the station."

"What for? Wait. You don't think—"

"I don't know what to think just yet, Mr. Biersovich. I simply want to gather all the information I can. So please inform her that she should arrange to come down to the West End station at her earliest convenience."

"OK." My head was swimming. And Lena wasn't going to like this.

THE APARTMENT in Chelsea was empty and no sign of Lena. Whatever her errand was, she needed to be done with it and get back to base.

While I was grazing through the fridge for a late lunch, Tina called. She sounded excited.

"I'm getting somewhere. The detective on the case is totally incompetent. Good thing I know what I'm doing."

"I thought you weren't allowed to work on it."

"I'm not. Well, not officially. But I had a chat with Melissa this morning. She's the one who was pistol-whipped and had to take some time off. She told me she's definitely decided not to return to the store. Too traumatic. She may need therapy."

"That's too bad."

"Anyway, she talked with this detective and he didn't seem real keen on following up. She told him the guy was wearing a ski mask and the only distinguishing marks on him were nail polish on his right hand."

"Nail polish?"

"You would think that would be an important detail, right? I mean, you come to the cosmetics counter, we're going to notice something like that," Tina said. "The detective didn't think that was significant. Maybe he's gay, he said. But I'm certain it's a clue, and I've got a hunch what it is."

"Female impersonator?"

"Only on his right hand. Not his left."

"But why—"

"I'll let you know when I have more info."

Well, that was a strange development. What sort of guy would wear nail polish but only on one hand? Didn't mean anything to me but Tina knew a lot about cosmetics, being the veteran that she was, and if anyone could get to the bottom of it, she could.

The afternoon was getting on and Lena was still a no-show. No call either. Her lack of cellphone was getting to be a real pain in the ass. I shot a couple of games of pool and then had a nice conversation with Emmie, who caught me up on the latest store gossip. I told her Tina had a line on the robbers. She said Salmon Foster, the vice president of finance and de facto boss of everyone at the store, seemed particularly agitated about something and just screamed every time he met with Jane. Again, I could give her no timetable on my return.

As I was about to call Joe T back and make another plea for release from my assignment, Freddie called.

"Just landed in London, bud. Can you pick me up?"

"What the hell? Tell me you didn't just crash my working trip again, Freddie."

"Hell, no, I'm working myself. Didn't I tell you about the piece I'm going to do on my uncle and the football thing? Jeez, Beers. I thought you were my friend, but every time I call you nowadays I get the third degree and—"

"Sorry, Freddie. I'm just a bit tense. We can't seem to wrap up this mission. It's always something. First the agent gets mugged, then one of the sellers goes missing, then he turns up dead—"

"Whoa, whoa, whoa. Did you just say dead?"

"Murdered, apparently. At least that's what it looked like."

"You saw the body?"

"Yeah. It was at the building we were touring—"

"Beers, I know you're getting tired of hearing me say this. But I have to say it anyway. You need to get yourself out of that job and back into reporting before *you're* the body on the floor."

Sigh. Freddie was right—I needed out of this dead-end, literally, job. But going back to the newspaper wasn't the path that would work for me. And there was no other obvious option.

"Freddie, I have to go. I need to find Lena—"

"Look, we'll talk about this when I see you. So can you come pick me up?"

"I don't have a car, Freddie. You're on your own."

"That's OK. I can take the train into the city. Just give me your address."

"You can't stay here, Freddie. We're not at a hotel, we're at someone's apartment."

"Apartment? I don't need a place to stay, Beers. I have a suite at the Savoy. That's where Sir Reggie is meeting me."

"You're really doing a story?"

"Beers, why don't you believe me? I do actually work for a living, and I haven't come across a dead body yet."

He had a point there, a pretty good one.

"Look, why don't you and Lena come over for dinner. I understand there's a nice restaurant in the hotel. Dinner on me."

"That would be a first."

"What about Vegas? I seem to recall I bought you a pretty nice meal on my winnings."

"Oh, right. Well, let me run it by Lena."

"OK, I'll call you when I hit the hotel."

Groan. Just what I needed to further gum up the works—Freddie. But with any luck at all, he would be busy interviewing his uncle and we'd be winging our way back across the pond before he knew it. Besides, there was really not much to do anymore. We had done all we could. At least, that was my theory.

When Lena finally breezed in an hour later, she was carting more shopping bags, as I expected. I told her the detective wanted her to visit the station. Her initial reaction: no damn way. With a little convincing that it wasn't optional, she agreed to go in the next morning, with her receipts accounting for her movements, showing she was shopping and unable to commit murder.

She was way more enthusiastic about dinner with Freddie than I thought she would be. Perhaps it was the allure of the Savoy, one of London's premier hotels. At any rate, when Freddie called back, he and Lena had a nice long chat and settled on a rendezvous time.

Lena ordered me to wear the best outfit I brought: my tweed jacket and a pair of khaki slacks. Sitting next to Lena in the cab on the way over—she was wearing the blue spaghetti-strap number and a sweater to hide the tattoo—I still felt underdressed.

"I thought you were going to return that dress," I said.

"Naw, I think it works OK," Lena replied. She was right, as usual.

18

Dinner was simply superb. Freddie and Lena opted for sautéed grouse, while I stuck with the Beef Wellington. The restaurant was one of those classics—dark wood paneling, ornate ceiling and chandeliers in abundance. The waiter gave me the evil eye, probably because I wasn't wearing a tie.

Freddie said he had a call from Tina before we arrived. She was asking for the name of a sportswriter. He surmised that she had run out of eligible cops to date.

He also explained his assignment in London: interview Sir Reggie on Saturday at the hotel, then take a helicopter ride down to his castle in Falmouth for an overnight visit before returning to London on Sunday, flying out Monday. Good. He would be too busy to meddle in our work, and with luck we would be gone before he returned to London.

Over dessert and coffee, I brought Freddie up to speed on our investigation of the two building sites. Before dinner, I had called Joe T to find out whether we could now arrange our trip back home. He said we had to wait until the renovator and architect had provided their estimates, then our job would be complete. I told him that could be a few more days. He said Vi would make sure their estimates were expedited, then she would book our flight.

"Who's this Vi character?" Freddie asked.

"Unsure," I said. "Works for Scalabrino, but I'm not certain in what capacity."

"She got a nice apawtment," Lena added. "Dat's wayah we stayin'." She described the place for Freddie, who said it sounded like the ideal living space, although he wouldn't want to pay the utility bill for a place that big. Lena also described Vi, which really made Freddie sit up and take notice.

"Sounds like just my type—female and good-looking. Maybe I can hang out with you guys tomorrow, shoot a little pool."

"No can do, Freddie. We have more work to do. This isn't a vacation."

"I know. I've got things to do Friday myself. A couple of interviews, some background stuff. Gotta look up those Vikings."

"Vikings?" Lena asked.

"Yeah, these guys kicking around the U.K., trying to get on an NFL Europe team. They were on the Vikings for about a half-minute, but hey, any local flavor I can get, y'know. That's how I sold the editor on this trip."

"Junket," I said.

"I'm working, Beers. Just because you never got to go anywhere nice when you were reporting—"

"I remain skeptical."

"I'll call you when the stories run so you can buy a paper. If you're nice, I'll autograph it for you."

Freddie did indeed pick up the tab, which ran to triple digits—in pounds. I was curious to find out how he would report that on his expenses.

Over my objections, Lena invited Freddie back to the apartment for a nightcap. And, of course, he accepted. He would never turn down a free drink.

On the cab ride back, I had a short conversation with Emmie. There was still nothing to report in the way of an ETA, but it was great to hear her voice again. She said Tina was in the store late in the afternoon and came to visit her. She had been talking with the other clerks on the first floor to see if she could pick up any more clues as to the identity of the robbers. No one in sportswear was very helpful, but she said she did get a little more info in cosmetics.

With a cab full of ears, we were unable to engage in our usual word foreplay. The ways I was going to ravish her on my return were piling up in my head.

When we arrived at the apartment building, Freddie wasn't impressed by its outward appearance. But he was blown away once we got inside, judging by the number of times he uttered "Wow!" as Lena led him through the rooms. Even though we had just finished downing a huge meal, he helped himself to some party tray goodies in the kitchen.

When he pulled out a cigar in the billiard parlor, that's where I drew the line. No stinky stogie here, I said. This isn't our place. He reluctantly agreed to curb his vice for the evening.

We shot pool for a bit and depleted the scotch stock to the best of our ability. Toward midnight, I was running out of steam and tiring of Freddie's non-stop banter. Lena was cackling at all his corny stories and putting away the wine like it was about to be outlawed.

At one point he described a business venture he planned to present to Sir Reggie—programmable shower heads that not only restricted the flow of water but also set the exact temperature. I asked how he planned to invent such a thing. He didn't know, but he thought his uncle might be willing to put an investment into the idea.

"Hare-brained scheme," I muttered.

"Again, you cut me to the quick," Freddie retorted. "You have a very low opinion of me sometimes, Beers. It makes me wonder if you're really my friend."

"I'm your friend, Freddie. But you need someone to rein you in. You're a loose cannon. I'm here to keep you from going off the rails. You should listen to my advice more."

"And wind up like you? No thanks, buddy."

Lena decided to take a shower, so I had to entertain Freddie solo for a spell.

"You ever have a weird dream, Beers?"

"No, never. They're all perfectly sensible and straightforward," I replied in my most sarcastic tone.

"Huh. That's strange."

"Of course I've had weird dreams. They're all weird!" I practically shouted.

"Oh. Well, I've got a theory about that..."

Here we go. Another of Freddie's wild-hair notions. He was becoming more eccentric with every day.

"Let's hear it."

"I've been reading up on dreams and what they mean. There are lots of ideas about what they really signify."

"Right. I get that."

"So...I'm thinking dreams aren't really dreams."

"Come again?"

"Well...what we think are dreams are in actual fact...actual fact."

"I'm not following."

"See, you spend eight hours a night in sleep mode, but in reality it's...reality. The dream part is when you're awake."

Even for Freddie, this theory was way out there.

"So what brought this on? I'm beginning to doubt your sanity, Freddie."

"Last night I dreamed I was flying. It's sort of a recurring dream."

"That's not so strange," I told him. "Weren't you on a plane?"

"No, not like that. Like I'm running real fast and I jump and suddenly I'm flying low over the ground. It seems pretty natural, like I've been doing it all my life."

"Freddie, I constantly have dreams about flying. It's normal." Although you're not very normal, I thought.

"The difference is..." Freddie didn't finish his thought.

"Yes? The difference is?"

"Well...I can really fly. I mean, it's the reality. When you think you're awake, you're really asleep. And vice versa."

"So I'm dreaming right now?"

"No."

"No? But I'm awake and you said—"

"You're not dreaming. I am. You don't really exist."

Now I was not only perplexed but flabbergasted.

"Freddie, nice chatting with you. but I've got a real life to live, so..."

"Just listen for a second. When I'm dreaming, it's so lifelike and real. When I'm awake, it sometimes seems like a dream. This whole world is nothing but part of my dreams. None of this exists in reality."

"So you're saying...I don't exist?"

"Just in my dream state."

"You know what? Maybe you need to dream that you're talking to someone else since I don't exist." I was fuming.

"Look, Beers, I didn't mean to piss you off."

"You're doing a pretty good job of it anyway. To someone who doesn't exist, apparently." I told him to call a cab and I'd see him back in Minneapolis. I was going to bed.

Before retiring, I made an entry in my notepad: Get Freddie to see a shrink. It sounded like he was crossing into a fantasy land from which there might be no return. Friend or no, he was treading on the thin ice of psychosis, and I didn't want to fall into that freezing lake with him.

19

My friend Freddie is what women consider a charming cad. I wouldn't know that except that one of his dates described him in those exact terms.

In the short time that I have known him, my five years in the Twin Cities, he has had approximately a hundred girlfriends. He wears them like a new pair of shoes for a week or so, then relegates them to the back of the closet. He rarely returns for a second go-round with a girl.

In contrast, I have had just three what I would consider steady girlfriends during that time—the girl I followed to Minneapolis (who shall remain nameless to protect my wounded ego); Rosie Sinfield, who had broken up with me as a result of my first close encounter with crime at La Scala; and the exquisitely lovely Emmie Slayton, whom I considered the crown jewel of womanhood. Freddie could have his short-term trysts; I had a keeper.

Sure, I had other dates but nothing that turned into more than a casual meet-and-greet, wine-and-dine or convenience escort. But I could count those on one hand, whereas Freddie would need hands, feet and a calculator.

Then there was Lena. I knew next to nothing about her love life. She kept it sealed inside a vacuum jar in a lock box in a bank vault. I thought I spotted her once dancing at a nightclub where I had gone to hear the band, but when I went looking for her, she had disappeared. If she had a regular boyfriend, or even a husband, I wouldn't know about it.

Unlike Freddie, Lena knew how to be discreet. And even though she had one brief fling with Freddie, she never spoke about it. Surprisingly, Freddie didn't either.

Tina, on the other hand, was an open book. Her dates usually were gleaned from the police corps. She loved a man in uniform. Or maybe it was because they spoke softly and carried a big nightstick. Whatever. She hadn't managed to find Patrolman Mr. Right either, although that didn't stop her from looking. Her frequency of hooking up with a new beau was almost in the Freddie league.

But getting back to Freddie, I am theorizing that his generally disjointed nature and tendency to go off half-cocked—absolutely no pun intended—is what contributes to his inability to commit to a long-term relationship. For him, long-term is two weeks. Well, he did have that girlfriend for a couple of months, a member of the U of M volleyball team, in my early days at the Herald.

As a matter of fact, now that I think about it, a large proportion of his dates seem to be coeds, and many of them athletes. I suppose his interview method always gets around to more personal information. A charming cad, indeed.

Maybe it was the dizzying array of personalities he was exposed to in his dalliances with the female persuasion that scrambled his brain.

As long as I've known him, he has targeted the younger members of the female set. OK, I admit a little guilt on that score myself. Emmie is young enough to be my...little sister. But at least she's in her 20s. Freddie's dates by and large are still in their teens.

I can recall an instance when he brought his newest conquest up to the office while he finished a recap of the Gopher football team's Friday practice. The young brunette sat on the corner of his desk chewing gum, blowing bubbles and yakking non-stop, much to the consternation of the assistant sports editor on duty. The guy was reluctant to evict her, however, seeing as she was wearing a very tight top and short-shorts, a visual most pleasing to the male eye.

I didn't really notice how frequently he went for the post-toddler age group until we double-dated one time. This was when I was still with Rosie, before the big dump. We went to a Gopher basketball game because his nephew was on the team. Athletic prowess doesn't seem to run in Freddie's family, however. Said nephew was one of the last scrubs off the bench in the final two minutes and even took the last shot. He missed.

Anyway, that wasn't the highlight of the evening. That started when Freddie was surrounded at halftime by no less than four cheerleaders who seemed to know him quite well. They cooed and giggled over him until his date insisted they visit the refreshment stand, an obvious ploy to escape the other hussies.

Then after the game, as we were leaving, one of the cheerleaders sidled up to lover boy, whereupon his date, who I forgot to mention was about five feet tall and looked like she was a middle-schooler, cold-cocked the young lass and was subsequently detained by campus police.

If I'm remembering correctly, she may have been the one he hung onto for a month, an eternity in Freddie dating time. Her name was Sindee. You always have to be cautious of people who insist on spelling their names in strange ways.

In general, maturity is in short supply when Freddie goes on a date.

Lord knows I've tried to steer him toward more stable relationships. I've even offered to fix him up with some women in his age bracket. He has always scoffed at my offers, however, insisting that I was an amateur when it came to hooking up with the opposite sex.

I suppose it's a small sign of maturity that Freddie hasn't tried to muscle in on my relationship with Emmie. Perhaps he has boundaries after all. But even though he's my friend, I wouldn't turn my back on him for long. I trust him but don't trust him. Charming cad or not, he has left too many discarded women in his wake.

20

Friday, April 13

I was up before Lena and had to make coffee. Glancing at the calendar, I saw it was Friday the 13th. Not a good omen.

The day started with no game plan, but that quickly changed when I spotted a note left by Vi. She obviously had come and gone during the night.

Our assignment was to find out when the building would be reopened to continue the survey. The architect apparently needed to revisit the site, since he had found a discrepancy in his measurements after getting a copy of the blueprints from the building inspector. Meanwhile, Vi would contact the family and diplomatically try to see whether a purchase agreement could be completed now.

When Lena straggled into the kitchen, I was on my third cup of coffee. She looked like she had been run over by a bulldozer and moaned through her first cup with her eyes closed. Finally, she opened her eyes and spoke.

"Jus' shoot me," she said.

"I had a bit to drink myself last night."

"Yeah, but you went ta bed roun' one, dintcha?"

"I took some ibuprofen before I went to sleep. Didn't you?"

"Yeah, but dat was roun' tree ayem. I hadda few moah aftah you went down. Freddie stayed late."

"Well, don't forget you need to go speak with the constable today."

She groaned. "Las' thing I wanna do." But she finished her coffee and hit the shower to try to sober up.

Vi's message left me with lots of questions, chief among them: When do we get to leave? I rang her and inquired. She said to leave the arrangements to her. We could likely depart within the next couple of days. She said the tear-down and renovation estimate on the apartment building came in way higher than feasible—4.2 million.

"Four million dollars?!" I asked.

"Pounds, dear. Way out of our price range. I suspect the estimate on the warehouse will be considerably less, in the one million range. But we need them to finish looking through the building to make sure there are no hidden defects that would spike the price."

"We have to go see the detective today, so I'll ask when they can get back in."

"And I just heard from the agent's office, Mr. Tilden? He said the first agent inquired about you."

"Charlene McAllen? How is she doing?"

"I didn't know about the mugging. He said she was doing much better and would be released in a few days. Perhaps you should go visit her."

Lena and I planned to do just that, following the chat with DC Huntington. Lena had the wherewithal to bring the receipts from her extended shopping spree, so Huntington quickly let her off the hook. He wasn't very forthcoming with the investigation, except to say that they were continuing to scour the building and talking with some key people. He said it might be possible to get back in the building Saturday if we had an officer escort us.

I waited until noon to call Joe T and give him the update. He already knew about the estimate on the first site and cursed about it. He told me to stick with the warehouse. Get the architect in Saturday and we might be able to come home Sunday, he said. Great news!

I dialed Naughton and told him to line up Greene for Saturday and I would arrange for the police to open the building. We agreed on 1 p.m. for the walk-through. Huntington was also agreeable to that time and told me he would send Officer Lindom as an escort for the inspection.

At the hospital, we were pointed toward the elevator and rode up to the seventh floor. Charlene was awake when we arrived, and Lena presented a bouquet of roses she had acquired from Safeway.

"How nice to see you again!" she said as we entered. There were bruises and healing scrapes on her face. A large bandage covered the right side of her scalp and her left arm was in a cast.

"We were so sorry to hear about...what happened to you. How are you feeling?" I asked.

"Oh, much better. Doctor says I'll be released in a few more days. Then just have to deal with this nasty cast and of course the headgear." She rolled her eyes and laughed.

"How's ya head?" Lena asked.

"Apart from the cracked skull? Never better," she said with a grin. "It's not so bad. Perhaps knocked some sense into me. Headaches have diminished greatly, thanks to the little pills they bring me."

"So I guess Mr. Tilden has brought you up to date on the building."

"No, as a matter of fact, I haven't heard a peep. What's the status? Do we have a purchase agreement?"

Lena and I glanced at each other. "Naw, what we got is a body," she said.

Charlene had a puzzled look, so I explained about the discovery of Stony Perkins' body as we were surveying the place, the shutdown by police and expected resumption on Saturday.

"Oh dear," she said. "Well, I do hope everything works out for you."

"Have the police got any leads on who assaulted you?"

"I'm afraid not. Those sorts of things never get solved. There are a hundred muggings in London every day."

"That's too bad."

"It's funny. This only came to me a couple of days ago. But just before I got bonked on the noggin, I heard someone say something about safe. Like, 'It's safe' or 'It's a safe.' Didn't make any sense to me. Still doesn't, now that I think about it."

"Was it the mugger who said that?"

"Not sure. Maybe. They were probably speaking with someone else."

"Did you tell the police?"

"No. They questioned me after the operation, and I told them I didn't see anything. I was still rather groggy from the anesthesia."

A nurse arrived to check on her so we said our goodbyes. Lena agreed to a late lunch back at my newly acquired old stomping grounds, Edgingham's. Cerise was back on duty, brought me the usual and Lena a pot pie.

"What's wit' da peas?" she asked, as I dug into my meal.

"Don't know. Tradition, I guess."

"Dey eat lotsa fish in Noo Awlins," she said, "but I ain't nevah seen anyone ordah a side a peas."

She told me she had just about completed her report on the history of the warehouse but needed to make one more trip to the library. Nothing was on my agenda, so a return foray to Mercy Beats seemed like the thing to do. We agreed to meet up for drinks in the apartment at 6.

I WAS ON my second pint of bitter at a pub down the road from Mercy Beats, reading the liner notes of my latest album purchase, when Freddie called.

"What is it, Freddie?"

"What kind of tone is that? I call you up to chat and you're all, 'Who have you stabbed now?'"

"Sorry. Sometimes I expect the worst."

"You could ask me about my day."

"How was your day?"

"I got two interviews done, most of a story written. Later I'm meeting my uncle. Should be very interesting."

"Sounds great."

"There is one thing..."

Here it comes, I thought. There was always a catch with Freddie.

"What?"

"I need to stay at your apartment."

"My apartment? In Minneapolis? You got evicted from your place?"

"No, I mean your apartment here. With the bar and the pool table."

"Are you fucking kidding me?"

"No, Beers, I'm not."

"I thought you had this fancy hotel suite."

"Did. Not anymore."

"What happened?"

"There was a misunderstanding..."

"What did you do?"

"Well, when I got in last night, I mean this morning, I sort of disassembled the shower head. The maid ratted on me."

"What the hell did you do that for?"

"For my invention. I wanted to see how it works."

"Freddie, I really think you're losing it. You need to seek immediate psychiatric help."

"Look, I just need a place to hang out for a while. I'm going to the castle this evening."

"Just hang out at the hotel."

"They don't want me here."

"Well, ride the Tube."

"I've got all this luggage."

"Aren't you meeting your uncle at the hotel?"

"I told him I found a nicer place to meet up."

"Don't tell me—the apartment we're staying at?"

"Bingo."

"Freddie, I...I don't know what to say."

"Just give me the address, and I'll be over there in a bit."

"I'm not there right now."

"I'll wait for you."

Typical Freddie. Gum up the works and have me bail him out. I was furious. Then after a couple minutes of reflection, I remembered that I had also been kicked out of a hotel. Of course, I didn't destroy any hotel property in the process.

21

I had just finished laying down the law to Freddie, including an admonition not to disassemble any hardware, when Lena walked in with a sheaf of papers.

"What's goin' on?" she asked.

"Meet our new squatter," I said. Freddie beamed at her.

"You gotta be kiddin' me!"

"Afraid not. It seems Mr. Knucklehead got himself thrown out of his hotel."

Lena gawked at Freddie, then slowly turned to me, grinning. "Theah's a lotta dat goin' round."

"I won't be any trouble," Freddie said. "Anyway, I'm leaving to go to my uncle's place later, so I'll hardly be here."

"Jus' pawk yaself ovah dere an' try not ta cause trouble."

"Can I fix a drink?"

"One," Lena said sternly. Freddie cheerfully wandered off to the bar.

"Find out any more about the building?" I asked.

"Yeah, got a bit moah stuff on da early nineteen hunneds. Dey had quite a bit a shenanigans wit' da title."

"How so?"

"Buncha lawsuits ovah ownahship. One guy claimed dis udda guy gave him da buildin', den reneged. Had a handwritten title. Udda guy said he was drunk when he signed it. Long fight in court. In da end, dey hadda split da title. Den one guy takes off fa pawts unknown, kinfolk file anuddah suit, yada yada yada."

"Good grief."

"Yeah. So long story shawt, old man Featherstonaugh buys da propahty befoah da war and starts sprucin' da place up."

"The family has clear title, correct?"

"Far as I can tell, yeah."

"How long do you have left to go on this stuff?" Freddie asked.

"Just about done, I hope." I crossed my fingers.

While waiting for Freddie to head off with his uncle, we shot pool. Lena stood in front of the bar with arms folded when Freddie tried to freshen his drink. She shook her head and stood her ground. Good move, I thought. Freddie looked hurt, but I think he understood that getting sloshed again wasn't in his best interest.

Jillian called and reported that her uncle was delighted with my progress so far in sorting out his accumulation of tunes. He would like me to come by and collect a reward, and advise him on displaying the collection. I did a little happy dance after hanging up.

Over sandwiches in the kitchen, I explained how I had sorted through the former deejay's piles of discs and tapes, turning a mishmash into a more manageable and valuable collection. This is exactly the type of job I'm most qualified for, I said. Good luck making a career out of that, Freddie retorted.

Tina phoned and said she was making real progress on the robbery investigation, without the assistance of either the police or the store's substitute security chief. She had spoken with another of the clerks on duty, who said the ski mask the robber was wearing had a ball on top, and it brushed the bottom of the Lancome sign. This told her the robber was five-ten at most.

Lena chatted with her a bit and I heard the name Raleigh mentioned again. This was the second time I had heard that name and it was bugging me. After they ended their conversation, I asked who's Raleigh. She just gave me that Cheshire grin again and left the kitchen.

The evening wore on and I was getting ready to head over to Jillian's uncle's place. Freddie still hadn't heard from Sir Reggie. As I was about to walk out the door, his phone rang. It was his uncle. They conversed for a few minutes, and Freddie had a glum look when he hung up.

"Tonight's off," he said.

"What happened?"

"Uncle Reggie said something came up. He'll have to come to London tomorrow."

Oh shit. I knew what was coming.

"So can I crash here tonight?" he asked.

"Freddie...no. No way. No how. No. We can't—"

"What's da problem?" Lena re-entered the billiard parlor.

"Sir Reggie is putting off our interview until tomorrow, and I've got no place to stay. So I was wondering if I could stay here, just for tonight."

"There's no way in hell—"

"Sure. We got lotsa room heah," Lena jumped in. She pointed toward the adjacent hallway in the south wing and said, "Find a room." He grabbed his gear and headed that way before I could stop him.

"Why did you do that?" I asked Lena.

"It'll be OK, Beers. Just chill. I'll keep an eye on him."

"You'd better. If we get evicted from here because of him..."

"He'll behave. Or else."

"Well, I have to go out for a bit so keep an eye on him."

"No can do, Beers. Goin' out myself."

"Well, we can't just leave him here unattended."

"Why not?" Lena asked.

"Because he's Freddie," I answered.

"Oh, yeah. Good point."

"You'll have to take him with you."

Lena laughed, said, "No," and walked off to her room.

Shitburgers. I certainly didn't want to baby-sit Freddie all night but it looked like I was stuck with him. There was no way I could leave him alone in the apartment.

So when the time came, he and I headed off to Lawrence Hickey's place. I warned him not to touch anything at least ten times. He promised he would be good.

Perhaps I should have had a premonition of the catastrophe to come. It was Friday the 13th, after all. My Freddie Early Warning System let me down.

Hick greeted us and said Jillian had a previous engagement. He offered tea, which I accepted. I placed Freddie on a couch and told him not to move. He promised he would sit quietly while I worked.

As Hick poured me a cup from a pewter teapot, I explained how he could set up shelves to display the collection, along with plate holders or disc racks to show off the most interesting items. He made notes. Then he wanted advice on what to do with the barrel of forty-fives. We moved down the short hall to the bedroom to consider it.

That's when we heard the crash.

Rushing back to the living room, we were aghast to see Freddie lying on the hardwood floor, sprawled among a now-scrambled sea of discs.

"Holy fuck, that's hot!" he yelled. There was a cup on the floor next to him and a puddle of tea in which sat a Tom Jones album, soaking up the liquid rapidly.

Hick and I were too stunned to speak.

I watched in horror as Freddie pushed himself up off the floor and stepped on a fanned-out pile of records. The snapping sound caused me to scream, "Don't move!"

"Sorry," he said sheepishly. He explained what happened: When we left the room, he poured himself a cup of tea, then walked over to examine the mountains of music. The tea burned his lip, which caused him to juggle the cup, which sloshed steaming hot liquid onto his hand, which led to him drop the cup, which then splashed the burning brew onto his pants, causing him to jump backward and knock into two piles of albums, which then knocked over other stacks in domino style.

Hick was still too stunned to speak. Not only was his newly ordered collection now in shambles but there obviously had been some damage in the aftermath. Although I apologized profusely and offered to sort the mess once again, Hick wouldn't hear of it. I think he wanted Freddie gone as soon as possible. Picking up on that, I hustled him out and called a cab.

Freddie was contrite on the way back and said he was sorry several times, explaining that he had no idea tea could be so hot. I was too angry to say anything.

It wasn't until we got into the apartment and Freddie asked if I was ever going to talk to him again that I responded: "You're a walking disaster area!"

And I got angry all over again when I realized I didn't collect my reward. There probably wouldn't be any reward after that fiasco.

22

Saturday, April 14

By the morning, I had cooled off somewhat. There were no overnight incidents that I was aware of, and Freddie had split bright and early so as not to further incur my wrath.

Part of my mellowing out was due to the fact that I just had to clear one more hurdle before heading back home to my honey. I dialed Vi to make sure she was handling the return ticket. She said there was a potential snag in that the siblings had not been able to get a go-ahead from Jasmine Sloane. She was refusing to talk to them. Unless Jasmine could be swayed, the whole deal would fall through.

That wasn't my job, I asserted. My task was to investigate the building and find out whether it fit the requirements for a full-fledged La Scala department store. The mission had changed, Vi said. Because this building was the only viable choice, the sale must go through, so Jasmine needed to be convinced. Since she wouldn't talk to the siblings, someone else would have to sway her. And that someone was me, seeing as I had met her and had already established a rapport.

"Bad timing," I said. "She's about to bury her husband."

"Common law," Vi replied.

"Whatever. Don't you think negotiating a sale right now is a bit...insensitive?"

"She's a widow now and needs money. I'm sure you can convince her this is the wise choice."

"But I don't—"

"Mr. Scalabrino says you have a way of getting things done. He has full faith in you. The funeral is at 3 p.m., Vale Cemetery."

"But I—"

"And after you speak with her, I'll get your return ticket lined up."

Well, that was the winning argument, right there. If it had to be done, I'd give it a shot, but I wasn't making any guarantees.

"Who was dat on da phone?" Lena staggered into the kitchen in her white silk nightgown, rubbing her eyes.

"Vi says I need to talk to Jasmine, try to convince her to sell."

"Huh. Dat's your job now?"

"Apparently so."

Lena agreed to meet up with the architect while I returned to Luton to attend the funeral. This wasn't going to be fun.

The bus trip back up to Luton was in a steady drizzle. Being unprepared for the weather, I purchased a "brolly" at the airport before catching a taxi to the cemetery.

A canopy had been set up at graveside with a dozen or so chairs for family. The siblings and their spouses were in the back row. A sobbing Jasmine was in the front row center, with the attorney, Beaton Dobbs, trying to comfort her. On either side were couples that I surmised were her siblings and their spouses.

Other attendees were standing outside the tent under umbrellas, so I figured it was gauche to crash the tent. Some ways off, under a tree, I spotted the sinister-looking Marston, smoking a cigarette. At the edge of the crowd stood a pair of police officers. I didn't know whether they were motorcycle escorts or were scanning the crowd for the killer.

"Poor Stony," a man next to me muttered. He looked to be late forties, early fifties, graying hair, wearing a camel hair blazer over a light blue shirt and dark slacks.

"It is a terrible tragedy," I said.

The guy looked at me.

"You a yank?"

"I'm from America, yes."

"How did you know Stony?"

"Never met him. Friend of Jasmine," I replied. "You a friend of Stony's?"

"He were my bud, yeah. It's the rest of them blighters what killed him off," he said with a sneer.

"Who?"

"Those lot in the back row," he replied.

"You think his siblings killed him?"

"Who else would it be then?"

"Do you have any evidence?"

"Plenty," he said, tapping his head with a finger.

"Have you told this to the authorities?"

He scoffed. "They had me in the nick yesterday. Told 'em what I'm telling you. I don't trust them brothers. Stony knew he were the black sheep."

The minister began prayers, and more sobbing could be heard from the crowd. Then he invited John Featherstonaugh to say a few words over the gravesite.

"My half-brother, Samuel Perkins—some of you knew him as Stony—was a kind soul and friend to everyone he met. He didn't have a lot, but what he had he gladly shared. I didn't know him very well growing up as there was a large age difference. But he took great care of our mother in her declining years..." Someone muttered, "Oh God," at this point. "...and had been a faithful companion to Jasmine." He gazed at her a few seconds and her crying grew louder. "I speak for the rest of my siblings when I say we will miss him tremendously." He ran out of words and concluded with "God bless Stony."

"Bollocks," the guy next to me growled. "He's just taking the piss."

Jasmine approached the casket and put a rose on top of it, then it was lowered into the ground. I spotted Marston grinding out his smoke and heading back to the car. Some of the crowd also drifted away, but the bobbies stood their ground.

It was now or never. I approached Jasmine and asked if I could speak with her sometime that afternoon. Beaton Dobbs intercepted me and said Jasmine needed to be alone right now. They headed off to the line of cars, with Dobbs supporting Jasmine. I watched until they drove off.

"You won't get anything out of that lot," a voice behind me said. It was the guy I was standing next to during the service. "Bunch of wankers."

"Davey. Davey Enthoven," he said, offering his hand. The name sounded familiar.

"Jim Biersovich. Friends call me Beers." He chuckled at that.

"Me and some of the boys are toasting old Stony down at pub, if you want to hoist a few beers, Beers," he said with a smile. That sounded like as good a plan as any at the moment. He offered a ride, which I accepted. After dropping his wife off at their home, we drove to the Luton Rathskeller, where tables had been pushed together, and a half-dozen men were already downing pints.

Davey introduced me to the group and bought a round. Then a man named Newt said, "You figgered out who done it, Davey?"

"I got me suspicions," he said with a grimace. "Old Stony were supposed to go out on a job with me Thursday, and he begged off. Said he had something to look into."

"Job? What sort of job?" I asked.

"Garden extension at the Williams estate."

"Ah, you're the landscaper, right?"

"That's right. Stony helped me out now and again. He didn't know nothing about gardening, but he knew how to take directions." Enthoven smiled and got quiet for a moment. "Stony was your typical hail-fellow-well-met."

"Meaning what?" I asked.

"A good bloke. A regular guy, you yanks would say. Mind you, he didn't have the ambitions of his siblings, which is why they considered him the black sheep. Money-grubbing bastards. It was all about the bunce for that lot. Always trying to make Stony take it up the bum. I think they was jealous of him, him being younger and with a beautiful woman and all. Anyhoo, so I never did find out what the mystery was about. Then poor old Stony turns up dead, don't he?"

There was general silence and lots of swigging after this.

"Poor old bugger," Newt muttered.

"This thing he had to look into—could it have something to do with the warehouse property? The building in London that the family has for sale? That's why I'm here, to examine the site for possible purchase."

"Don't know," Enthoven said. "He might have been off on a lark with Tom-Tom."

"Who's Tom-Tom?"

"Sometimes bandmate. They would play odd gigs, clubs and the sort. Nickname is Buckets. Plays the drums."

"What's his last name?"

"Can't say. But I can tell you this. Stony weren't keen to sell that building. It had sentimental value, he told me. There was something about it that made him want to hang onto it. Course, those other toe-rags what called him brother would sell their mum for a quid, wouldn't they?"

"And you think that's why Stony was...because he didn't want to sell?"

Enthoven just looked at me and downed the rest of his mug. Another man signaled for the next round and general chatter broke out. The tales of Stony the sometimes barmy character started flowing. None of them seemed a more likely cause for his dispatch than the impasse over sale of the warehouse.

Which put his siblings square in the spotlight of most likely suspects.

23

Lena's phone call ended my drinking. The architect had been trailed through the building by a police officer as he completed his measurements. She said on the first floor, as he was kneeling with his tape measure against the wall, he muttered, "Indeed strange." Then he knocked on the back wall for five minutes. She couldn't tell me what that meant, but the architect promised a full report in a day or two.

My journey to Luton had been unproductive, outside of a couple of free beers. Since Jasmine didn't want to speak to me, I decided I had to at least make an effort with her attorney. I found a phone booth in the pub hallway and looked up the number in the book. He agreed to meet me in a half-hour, so I called a taxi.

The group showed no signs of slowing down. I offered my glad-to-meet-yous, gave Enthoven my card, scribbled my temporary number on it and headed to the curb. I arrived at Dobbs' office 15 minutes before he showed up, which gave me time to glance through my notes and look for any anomalies. Nothing.

Dobbs ushered me in and showed me to a chair across from his desk. He said he could give me a few minutes before heading off to another engagement.

"I need to speak with Jasmine about the warehouse property," I said.

"As you can understand, she's not in a frame of mind to discuss business at the moment. I suggest you come back in a week or two, when the shock of old Stony's passing has eased a bit."

Panic. "No. Can't do that. I need to leave London in the next day or two."

"Well, I'm afraid speaking with Jasmine is out of the question." He leaned back in his big leather chair and folded his hands across his ample midsection.

"Do you have any idea why Jasmine...and Stony...should be opposed to selling it?"

"No clue." He smiled at me.

"Perhaps you could ask Jasmine for me."

"No, I'm afraid not. Now if there's anything else...?"

He wasn't budging. I thought about trying an end-around and going back to Jasmine's cottage, but that would be pretty insensitive so soon after she buried her husband. This was a dead end. So to speak.

Dobbs offered a ride back to the airport and I accepted. His jade green Jaguar had a vanity plate that included his nickname: BE22 ANY.

At the airport while waiting for the bus back to London, I called Vi and reported on my failure to see Jasmine. She was adamant that I at least try, bypassing the solicitor if necessary. Insensitive or not, Jasmine must be asked about her intent to sell. Either that or hang around until she's ready to talk, Vi said.

There was no way in hell I wanted to remain in the U.K. for another week or two, so I grabbed a taxi back into town. A wreath hung on the door to Jasmine Sloane's cottage. I knocked, and a woman I hadn't seen before answered.

"Hi, I'm Jim Biersovich. A friend of Jasmine. Could I speak with her a moment?"

The lady introduced herself as Mrs. Trimble, Jasmine's neighbor, and said she was resting and shouldn't be disturbed. As I was about to leave, I heard, "It's OK, Maggie," and the door opened wider. Jasmine was in the attire I had seen before—jeans and an old sweatshirt.

They ushered me in and Mrs. Trimble said she would put on a kettle. While she was in the kitchen, Jasmine went to a cabinet and pulled out a bottle of scotch and a glass, sat on the chair across from mine and poured two fingers, which she promptly downed.

"Sorry," she said. "Fancy a bevvy?" I declined.

"I just wanted to say how sorry I was to learn about Stony's...passing." He had gotten help in passing, but I wasn't going to mention that.

She sighed heavily. "Stony and me, we had our ups and downs, but I know he loved me."

"You know, I was one of the people that found...Stony. We were touring the building—"

Mrs. Trimble entered with the tea on a tray and set it down on the low table between us.

"Thank you, Maggie. I'll talk with you tomorrow," Jasmine said.

"If you need me to—"

"I'll see you tomorrow, love." Mrs. Trimble gathered her coat and left.

"Can you help me?" Jasmine asked.

"Help you how?"

"Find out who did him in."

Here we go again, I thought. Asked to step into the middle of a criminal case more properly conducted by police. Her eyes were pleading. There was a lot I could read into her gaze, a vulnerability that stirred in me a desire to assist.

"I don't know what I can do," I replied. "Have you spoken to the authorities?"

She ignored her tea and poured another drink. "Fat lot of good that does. Stony...he was sometimes on the outs with those chaps."

"How so?"

She stood and walked toward the fireplace, pointed to one of the photos on the wall. "We were in Aruba when this was taken. Those were good times. Stony didn't care a dram about the family business. He went along with whatever his brothers and sister wanted. And so did I.

"He had what you call a varied career. At times he worked construction, sold property, tended bar, worked as a landscaper's helper, did a bit of importing. Couple of times he would go off for a few days, no call, then come back with a bankroll, said he made a nice sale. I never knew what he was selling and didn't ask. He told me what I needed to know, said he would handle the rest.

"But he was faithful to me, that I know. It wasn't like he went off and had some tart in Liverpool. We didn't have much, but he always provided."

"I don't know how much you know about...the situation." Had to tread lightly here. "Stony was found in the warehouse."

"I know about that."

"He was in a room where the wall was being broken up. You have any idea why that could be?"

"No, I don't."

"That's the building my boss is interested in purchasing. And Stony didn't want to sell. At least that's what his siblings told me."

"They would be correct."

"Any idea why?"

She downed the rest of her drink. "He didn't say specifically. He just said he wanted to hold up because he needed to check something out. They were pressuring him to sign off his rights, like all the other times. But this time, he said no."

"What was he looking for?"

She shook her head. "He had his reason. I don't know what that was, but I'm going along with him even though he's...gone."

"Mr. Enthoven mentioned a friend of Stony. Tom-Tom. Name ring a bell?"

"Tom-Tom? One of his bandmates, I believe. Only met him a couple of times. Seemed like a good bloke."

"Know his last name?"

Jasmine thought for a moment. "Walters? Walker? Something like that."

We sat in silence for a moment, she drinking scotch and me sipping tea. Then there was a knock at the front door. She asked me to see who it was. When I opened the door, I came face to face with Beaton Dobbs, who looked stunned to see me. His expression changed, and he got red in the face.

"You! What are you doing here? Get out!" he yelled.

"Miss Sloane invited me—"

"Get out, damn you! I told you not to disturb her!" He pushed past me into the living room and addressed Jasmine. "Are you all right, dear? Has this man been bothering you?"

Jasmine looked up wearily and said, "It's all right, Beany. Mr. Beers wants to help me."

Well, it apparently wasn't all right with Beany, because before I could react, he punched me square in the nose. It hurt like a sonofabitch, and blood started pouring down.

Jasmine was appalled and pushed Dobbs aside, then rushed to the kitchen to bring me a towel. She sat me down and had me put my head back while applying pressure.

In time, the bleeding stopped, but my shirt front and jacket were a mess.

"Sorry, old chap, but you see, I'm very protective of Jasmine...Miss Sloane's interests."

"Beany, you should go," Jasmine said.

"But I just wanted—"

"Just go," she said wearily. "I'll ring you tomorrow." He reluctantly left after staring at me a moment, like he wanted to follow up with an uppercut.

"I should go too," I told her.

"Are you OK? I don't know what got into Beany. He's been on edge for the last few days."

"What for?"

"I don't know. He must have picked it up from Stony." She paused and looked down at her hands, which she was wringing agitatedly. "Stony was...nervous about something. The last week or so. I could tell something was on his mind. He didn't tell me what, but he fidgeted around the house, locked himself in the loo for long periods. Went out but didn't come home with alcohol on his breath or anything of the sort. I felt he would tell me what was going on when he was good and ready."

"He didn't provide any clue to what it was?" I asked.

"No. Although there was something. I saw his mum's diary laying about one day."

"Diary?"

"He and his mum were close in her last years. Stony got a few keepsakes when she passed. He took her diary, said he was going to read it and find out what her life was like in the old days. But it was just stuffed in a trunk with all her other keepsakes for years. He never brought it out, so far as I know. Until last week. That's when I saw it."

"You didn't read it?"

"No. Didn't see Stony reading it either, but obviously he had. He only said his mum was a saint." She stopped talking and started to pour herself another scotch, but reconsidered and put the bottle down. "There was one strange thing...Stony said his mother always told him that old warehouse was his future, that he could bank on it."

"Did he say why?"

"No." She smiled. "He said he used to play in it when he was a kid. Run around in that big warehouse, look up at the high ceiling and pretend he was an astronaut. But that may be why he didn't want to sell it. Maybe he was meant to reopen the building, make a go of it. Steady job and all that. That was so unlike Stony."

"And where is this diary now?"

"Can't seem to find it."

"Well, if you do locate it, I would love to see what he found so compelling in there." I stood to go.

"There was one other thing," Jasmine said. "He said his father had left him a key marked with G."

"Where is this key?"

"I have no idea."

"What does the G stand for?"

"Again, no idea."

24

Jasmine insisted I take one of Stony's old shirts. She indicated she was going to send out my shirt and jacket for overnight cleaning, and they would be delivered to me in London in the morning. I resisted until she said she would send Beany the bill.

I thought it best to check in with Vi one more time before leaving Luton, in case there was another wild goose chase I was assigned. Surprisingly, she was delighted to get my report and muttered "Very interesting" several times. She concurred with my opinion that sale would be precluded until we found out exactly what Stony saw in that building. On the bright side, she agreed to line up return tickets for Lena and me and would call when all was arranged.

When I dialed the apartment number, Freddie answered. Curse words zipped into my head until he told me Lena had received a call and left in a hurry. He didn't know where she was going. Perhaps Vi sent *her* on a wild goose chase.

I asked Freddie what happened to the castle adventure. He said it was a long story that he would tell me over a drink when I returned.

The bus ride back to London gave me a chance to check in with Emmie and let her know that at long last it looked like I would be winging my way back to her arms. She was glad to hear that. She missed me as much as I missed her. She also told me she saw Tina, who looked quite excited about something but wouldn't say what. Could she have been rehired in cosmetics, I asked. Emmie didn't know.

I didn't bother calling Joe T to provide an update because I was certain Vi would do that. She seemed to have a pipeline into the inner sanctum. I was still curious to discover her role in the whole scheme of things.

Tina was on a stakeout when I called. This was a surprise.

"I thought you were pulling crap assignments."

"This is unofficial," she said. "I'm following this guy. Remember I told you about how I talked with the girls at the counter and got some more details about the perp?"

"Yeah, the fingernail polish."

"The fingernail polish is the key. When I checked on the progress of the case, the detective in charge didn't consider it significant. He said lots of cross dressers turn to crime. It's not a cross dresser, though."

"How do you know?"

"Because I'm watching this guy right now. He's making the rounds around Lake Street, meeting with some known gang bangers. I'm pretty certain this is the guy. Just need one more piece—hold on. Let me call you back." She cut the connection before I could inquire about her return to the civilian workforce.

Freddie had already gotten a head start on the drinking when I arrived. Lena was in the office on the computer, he said, so I headed that way.

"What's up, Lena?"

"How was ya trip up ta Luton?" she asked, maintaining a focus on the screen as she banged away at the keyboard.

"Stood in the rain at the funeral. Hoisted a few with the dearly departed's buddies. Spoke with the widow. Got punched in the nose." Lena finally looked up.

"Punched?"

"The lawyer. Seems he objected to me chatting with Jasmine."

"Wheredja get dat shirt?"

"Mine had some blood on it so Jasmine gave me this to wear. Guess it was Stony's."

She shook her head, then went back to pecking on the keys.

"So tell me what happened at the warehouse."

"You not gonna believe dis," she said. "Greene got in dere and was measurin' da first floah. Said sumpin was wrong wit' da figyahs. Said he hadda check sumpin out an' would call me. So he did an' I went ovah dere and he showed me his sketch ovahlaid wit' da blueprints."

"And?"

"Didn't match up. Got a hidden back wall on one side."

"What does that mean?"

"Somewayah along da line, dey moved da back wall forwahd 'bout four feet. Dere's a trapped space."

"I don't get it."

"He didn't eithah. Said he hadda open up dat back wall to see why dey did dat. He's gonna check wit' da police an' da Featherstonaughs an' see if he can do dat."

Lena continued her computer search for some clue as to why or when the fake wall was constructed. Meanwhile, I had a Freddie to confront.

I was starving, so I fixed a party plate in the kitchen and grabbed a beer before heading into the pool room.

"I know what you're gonna say, so let me just explain," he started.

I quietly enjoyed my munchies and brew.

"So I finally met my uncle, Sir Reggie. He landed at the Vanguard Helipad, where a limo picked me up and took us to lunch at some restaurant called Inside. It was actually quite good, but everything had goat cheese on it.

"Anyway, we got to talking and he said he only had a short time to chat because he was flying off to Tierra del Fuego. There was a hiking expedition he was keen to join. I would have to join him at the castle some other time.

"Then I started quizzing him about the NFL Europe franchise he was pushing for, and he said that was a non-starter. He's already scrapped that idea, so I essentially have no story. My editor is going to shit a brick."

"Sorry about that, Fredster."

"And to top it all off, he had no interest whatsoever in my shower invention."

"It's not like you invented anything anyway."

"I have the idea. Big money guys like him have teams of fabricators that can whip up prototypes overnight."

"Doubtful."

"Irregardless, I got nothing. If I don't come up with a story, this trip is a disaster. They're going to make me pay for it."

"What about the guys you mentioned, used to play for the Vikings?"

"Also a bust. One's in prison and the other went to Belgium. Seems they were too out of shape to make a team, even in Europe. The coach they tried out for called them timid. Apparently, they were incapable of delivering a forearm shiver, an accepted form of punishment on the European fields of play."

He stopped for a moment. "Look, I know you're still pissed at me about the records."

"Freddie, that's the least of my worries right now." Actually, now that he brought it up, it made me mad all over again. Freddie has a way of doing that.

"I'm gonna make it up to you somehow. Let me help you with whatever it is you're working on. You know I'll come through for you, like all the other times."

"When have you come through for me?" I asked.

"How about Las Vegas? You said I had the idea that made all the pieces fall into place."

"That was a song, not an idea."

"Whatever. My song solved it for you."

"I'm not having this discussion right now. Besides, we're about to fly out of here, maybe tomorrow."

"My flight isn't until Wednesday. I suppose I could get it changed..."

"You'd better come up with a story idea for your editor or your ass is grass."

"Good point. Maybe he'd be interested in a mountain climbing expedition. I'll give him a call." Freddie downed the rest of his drink and scooted off toward his room.

It was still early afternoon back in Minneapolis, so it was prime time to evaluate happenings there. I had been avoiding talking to my dad but figured it was a good time to check on him.

Being fully retired once again, he had time to devote to his expansive pepper garden, renowned in his neighborhood of Highland Park, and his deepening relationship with my former boss, Jane. It was not the kind of thing I wanted to hear details about, and he was acceptably discreet. I gave him sketchy details of my time in London and promised to visit when I returned home.

While waiting around for Vi to call with information about our itinerary, I browsed the library tomes. I expected a heavy concentration of biographies and serious works but found a large number of popular fiction titles among the collection, including an entire shelf of bodice rippers.

That's when Lena located me and said she may have found the smoking gun.

Lena had already documented the various changes the building had undergone through the years. But now she discovered what she thought was an unauthorized renovation during World War II. That's when the back wall was moved up a few feet, she speculated. Why, she had no clue, but she was going to call the architect first thing in the morning.

25

Sunday, April 15

Finally going home, I thought as I woke up to another foggy morning. This would be a day for wrapping up loose ends and saying goodbye to London, to my new friend at the record shop and enjoying a last lunch of fish 'n' chips.

Oh, so naive.

John Lennon's wisdom comes to mind: *Life is what happens while you're busy making other plans.*

Freddie's effort to latch onto a secondary junket had been denied, so he was stuck in London a few more days with no viable prospects of salvaging his assignment.

I didn't want to be a pest—Freddie was the expert in that department—but I was antsy about the return flight. After waiting till a reasonable hour, I rang Vi to see whether she had our tickets. Predictably, there was another snag. "Johnny" would like me to take one more run at securing Jasmine's consent to sell. Apparently, she was on a first-name basis with the boss. But I guess that didn't mean much since he constantly told peons like me to call him Johnny.

"How exactly should I do that?" I asked. "This is a woman in mourning, being advised by her lawyer not to do anything. And she's on the outs with the rest of the family. It could take months, years to get her to agree to sell."

"Johnny says you have magical ways of getting things done," she replied. "I'm going on his belief in you."

"Belief in me? I don't believe in myself. I'm out of my depth here. I'm not trained for this type of negotiation."

129

"One more try. I promise this will be the last go. Then you and Miss Fangeaux can return home."

Grrrrr. I wasn't happy about this, but one more try it would have to be. And she promised, so maybe she would keep her word. I asked whether I would have to go all the way back up to Luton. She said a phone conversation would suffice. Good. A call, a quick turndown, and I'd be home free.

Again, wishful thinking fueled by desire does not alter fate.

Lena rushed out of her room on the way out the door. All she had time to tell me was she was meeting with the architect again. I was starting to think she had a thing going on with him, which might mean at least one person was getting somewhere in London.

When I rang Jasmine Sloane's number, Mrs. Trimble answered and said Jasmine had just been admitted to the Luton and Dunstable Hospital. Nothing serious, she said, but Jasmine was suffering fatigue. No visitors at this time. Great.

Then I decided the next best thing was to call Beaton Dobbs, give him a chance to apologize for the poke or at least act a bit more civil. This time, I wasn't disappointed.

"Sorry about that, old chap. But Jasmine is a delicate flower. Stony and I go back a ways. I feel obligated to protect her." It made me think he had the hots for her.

"I understand she's hospitalized."

"Just precautionary. I think all this..." He paused, looking for the right word. "...commotion has her in a state."

"Well, I just wanted to ask her one more time about the warehouse property."

"Afraid not. You see, Stony had a strong desire to keep it in the family."

"But the rest of the family wants to get rid of it," I argued.

"They'll come to their senses in time."

How would that come about, I thought. Certainly they wouldn't listen to Jasmine, given their general disdain for her.

"So you're saying there's no way ever that she's going to agree to a sale? There's no price high enough?"

"Not necessarily. Just at this moment in time...well, things have to play out."

Things? What things? I wondered.

This was going nowhere. I said goodbye and wondered how to deliver the news to Vi. Johnny wasn't going to like it, but it looked like his dream of a U.K. store would have to be put on hold, unless he could locate some other site.

The topper was a call to Tilden, during which I reported that all attempts at lining up a willing seller seemed to be doomed. He responded that the gods were angry, and their luck was on the skids, because the body of a vagrant had been discovered in the closed-up apartment building after the comic book proprietor noticed a foul odor. Now that location was also wrapped in yellow tape.

What the hell was going on in jolly olde London? The body count was rising, and the previously promised hassle-free scouting trip was turning into "Crime Story."

I could call Vi and report the bad news, but she would probably come up with another "one more thing" for me to attempt. Lena wasn't around, Freddie was God knows where, and I didn't feel like thinking any more about Mission Improbable. There was only one thing to do: Hit the Tube and continue my musical quest. Screw everything.

Back up to Portobello Road I went, to my now favorite record shop, Mercy Beats. It was closed. Being a Sunday, it opened at 1 p.m. I had time to kill and where better than a pub. Wandering through the neighborhood, I found a heretofore unvisited spot and popped in for lunch and a pint.

As I was spearing the last pea, Freddie called. He was despondent, without a lead and facing the prospect of reimbursing the paper for his trip.

"I've got to have a story or I'm dead," he said. "So I was thinking...what if I wrote about your trip here to look for a store site for La Scala? It would be the perfect thing. Local angle, intrigue, murder—"

"Are you insane, Freddie? You can't write about that. Besides, it's not a sports story."

"Well...I can write a feature, y'know. Doesn't have to be sports."

"No way. Scalabrino would drop-kick me over the moon if all this got in the paper. And you'd wind up under Hidden Falls with broken kneecaps."

He contemplated that a second. "So he *is* in the Mafia. Is that what you're saying?"

"Freddie, just drop it. You're not writing about La Scala. You may as well just go home and face the music."

"You're a big help."

"I'm not the one who lined up a junket without a Plan B," I said.

"They'll crucify me for this," Freddie moaned.

"I gotta go. Good luck." I hung up and finished my beer, then moseyed back down to the shop.

When I inquired about Jillian, the clerk on duty said she was off. I thought about ringing her and trying to see her uncle again, but that ship had already sailed, most likely. Thanks again, Freddie.

The pickings were slim, and I was just leaving the store when Lena called. We had another problem she didn't want to talk about over the phone. But I needed to get down to the warehouse pronto.

All sorts of scenarios played through my head as I rode the Tube, none of them pleasant. And the most dreadful thought of all—we would be held over in London yet again.

Roger Miller might have sung about "bobbies on bicycles, two by two," but I hadn't seen a single one pedaling through London. When I emerged from the Tube station and heard that telltale EE-O-EE-O-EE-O sound you hear in the movies, I knew something bad had happened.

Arriving at the building, I spotted three police cars at the curb with sirens wailing and a small crowd gathered on the sidewalk.

"What's happening?" I asked the man nearest me.

"Bloody Armageddon, if you ask me," he responded.

Police weren't letting anyone near the entrance. In time, paramedics came out rolling a gurney on which lay a sheet-draped body. My heart jumped into my throat as I feared that Lena had been injured or, worse, killed. But a few seconds later I heard that magnificent New Orleans patois as she walked out with a couple of officers, explaining why she was there.

"...so when he called, I got ovah heah ta look at da wall he hadda question about. Dat's when I found him."

"Lena!" I yelled at her. She looked up and rushed over to me. "You OK? What happened? Is that a..."

"Croaked. Da awkiteck, Greene. Tell ya all about it, but I gotta go down ta da West End station an' give a statement first." She walked back over to the officers, who escorted her to a patrol car.

"I'll meet you there," I yelled before the door closed on her. I hit the Tube again and headed for the station.

26

The coffee in the police station was terrible. I waited around on a bench in the intake area for almost two hours while Lena was grilled. They were probably putting bamboo shoots under her nails. I was certain her accent was a major stumbling block.

Finally, she emerged with a grim look and said the constable wanted a word with me.

Detective Constable Huntington was seated behind his desk with a pair of young coppers standing beside it.

"Constable," I said. We sat in the chairs across from him.

"Mr. Biersovich," he replied, looking first at me, then Lena. "Want to tell me what's going on?"

Lena jumped in. "Like I said, I was waitin' fa da awkiteck ta show up. He had sumpin ta tell me 'bout da plans fa da buildin,' " she began.

"I'd like to hear Mr. Biersovich's story," he replied.

"Well...what she said," I responded.

"I see," Huntington said. "Was there anyone else there?"

"Not dat I could see. Door was open so I went in...found him dead."

"Who unlocked the building?" Huntington asked.

Lena shrugged.

"We were working with an estate agent, Charlene McAllen. She was mugged a few days ago. So another agent took over, Mr. Tilden. He may have opened it."

"Didn't see him dere, Beers."

"You were there to witness the first death."

"Are you talking about the vagrant? Because I didn't witness anything. We discovered him already dead."

"Autopsy shows he was also murdered, with a blow to the head. You don't know anything about that, I suppose."

"Not a thing. Like I said—"

"Thomas Waters. Name doesn't ring a bell?" he asked.

"I have no idea who that is."

Huntington sat silently for a minute and looked through some papers on his desk. Then he looked up and said, "You'll be going back to the States soon, Mr. Biersovich? Because I believe our citizenry will be safer when you've concluded your holiday."

"Now, wait a minute—"

He held up a hand and gave me another stern look, then expressed his hope that we have a safe flight back to America. In the meantime, he said, should we remember any other pertinent information, we were to bring it immediately to his attention. And by all means stay away from the warehouse building.

"But we're supposed to be having it evaluated for possible purchase," I argued.

"That's as may be, but it will remain closed for now," he countered.

Our strategy needed rethinking. Exiting the police station, I called Joe T, who was on his way to the Minneapolis store to deal with an issue.

"What's going on at the store?" I asked.

"First tell me what's happening there," Joe T countered. I brought him up to speed. He indicated we should continue to pursue the site by contacting the owners again. I thought that was a mistake but he was adamant.

Then he filled me in on the events at the store. Scalabrino was rethinking the security detail in light of the recent robbery. He was considering making Roger Thompson's assignment permanent and bringing on Detective Cuccia as an in-store presence. Also, he thought assigning me as Foster's assistant might make more sense.

I went ballistic.

"What the fuck does he want to do that for??!!" I yelled.

"Calm down, Jim. You're not here, we need help. That's all."

"I should be there! Not Thompson!" I was fuming. Here I was stuck in another murder case—not my own choosing—and instead of being called home to take care of my primary responsibility, I was floundering in a foreign land, dealing with a situation I had no business being involved in, missing my music and my lovely Emmie.

"What's going on, chief?" Lena asked when she heard my outburst.

"Nothing!" I yelled at her. Then back at Joe T: "I want to come home now. I can't handle this anymore. Johnny Scalabrino needs a SWAT team, not a security chief!"

"Calm down. And sit tight. Things will work out," Joe T responded.

"And that's another thing. I'm tired of sitting tight. Every time I do, someone dies!"

"You're exaggerating," he said. "Just keep your head. I'll talk to Johnny and get back to you." He hung up.

Lena looked at me expectantly. "Well?"

"He wants me to sit tight. Wait for instructions."

"Whatcha want me ta do, chief?" Lena glared at me.

"I don't know!" I yelled. It was the first time I can recall ever raising my voice to Lena. Obviously, my frustration was bubbling over and I lashed out at her undeservedly.

She stared at me a while, then flicked her hand. "You call me when ya figger it out, yeah?" And she turned to go. I could tell she was furious, but so was I. The job was getting to me. The pressure of responsibility. It suddenly became a burden, more so than the times previously that I was saving Scalabrino's empire from murderers and thieves.

I needed to calm down, clear my head. Usually when that was the case, I headed to The Crater, my frequent haunt in downtown Minneapolis. The barkeep, Sam, is a good listener when I need it. Even Freddie, at times, provides an adequate sounding board, when he isn't going off the deep end with one of his cockamamie theories.

In London, I didn't have The Crater or a Sam. But I did have a fully stocked bar back at the apartment. I hurried up the sidewalk to catch up with Lena.

We walked silently to the Tube station. Lena was mum all through the ride, and it wasn't until we got into the apartment with the door closed that we spoke.

"Sorry about that, Lena. The pressure is getting to me."

"Hacked," she said.

"Hacked?"

"Greene. Hacked wit' a machete or sumpin like dat. He called me ta meet him at da buildin' and I went ovah dere. Door was open. Didn't see him. Called out, no answer. Went lookin', found him in one a da back awfisses. Big crack in his skull. Like he been hacked wit' sumpin."

"No murder weapon?"

"Not dat I saw."

"How long between the time you talked to him and when you arrived at the building?"

"Oh, 'bout...twenny minutes? Long enough to get whacked."

I considered that for a moment.

"What da hell is goin' on heah?" Lena asked.

"I don't know, but I'm certain that building has a secret we haven't discovered yet."

"No lie."

This job was becoming dangerous. Whether it was a viable hazard to us remained to be seen, but I didn't really want to stick around to find out. Once more it was time to plead for release from the assignment.

Vi was appalled when I related the latest killing. But she agreed that it was becoming unsafe to continue and promised to get the tickets that day.

While I was throwing stuff in my suitcase, Freddie called. He was striking out in story land.

"I gotta have something. What about that record guy?"

"Record guy?"

"You know, the one with the stacks of albums and tapes."

"Oh, no way. You single-handedly destroyed his collection last time I was there."

"Look, I don't need you to go. Just give me his name, phone number, something."

"He won't let you within a fortnight of his stuff," I asserted.

"I have to at least try. C'mon, be a pal."

That was the argument that won me over. I hadn't been a pal to Freddie lately, just treated him like a major pest. Well, in my defense, he had been acting like one. But I decided to throw him a bone and gave him the number. Fat chance it would amount to more than a curt turndown.

Bag packed, I parked it in the game room and fixed myself a well-earned vodka rocks. I would much rather have been out downing a last taste of fish 'n' chips and a pint of bitter, but I didn't want one more thing to delay departure. At the bottom of my glass, I got up to refresh it, wondering why Vi hadn't rung with our itinerary. I also wondered why Lena was taking so long to pack.

Down the hall I went to check on her. She wasn't in her bedroom packing, though. She was back at the computer, absorbed in another research session. She didn't notice me until I called her name a second time.

"Oh, hey, Beers. Ya might wanna look at dis heah." She was indicating the computer screen.

"Why aren't you packing?"

She looked back at me. "I can't go nowhere. Police said stick around case dey had moah questions."

Damnit! Another snag in the exodus plan. At this rate, I might as well apply for permanent resident status.

Lena turned back to the screen and pointed to a map she had found on the web. It was a 1948 schematic of underground tunnels. The one she was pointing to went directly under the current location of the warehouse.

She couldn't explain exactly what it was for—speculated it was created during World War II when London was under siege from the Germans—but thought there was some connection with what was going on. Somewhere in the basement, she said, there was a hidden doorway to this tunnel that was used by the killer.

I asked how she knew that. She just shrugged. So she was guessing.

While I was trying to determine how I could leave and let Lena catch a later flight, Tina called. She was excited—she had nailed the robbers.

"No thanks to the detective in charge," she said. "I figured this one out by myself. Well, I had a little help. You remember I told you about what the clerks said? That the guy was wearing nail polish on one hand and he had a ski mask on and so forth? I remembered something from when I went down to Florida a couple years ago for the Twins' spring training.

"The catchers had nail polish on the fingers of their throwing hand. That's so the pitcher can see the signs easier. That would explain why this guy had polish on only one hand. So I guessed it was a catcher. The Twins were in Florida at the time, but the Saint Paul Saints had already broken camp.

"Freddie gave me the name of the sportswriter who covers the Saints. He agreed to help me on this. So he went over to the park under the pretense of doing a story on the players trying out for catcher. He got their vitals. One was the perfect height—one Hermano Gomez. I followed him around for a couple of days during my off hours. He hung with a rough crowd.

"The kicker was the night I trailed him to a liquor store in the Lake Street area. He was with another guy. They parked at the edge of the lot, donned ski masks and went in to rob the place. I called it in and blocked their getaway car. They were carrying pistols but no ammo, fortunately. Hermano and his partner in crime ratted each other out to try to cut a deal."

"Wow. Good job!"

"You don't have to be a detective to be a detective. As you know," she said.

"So is there a chance they'll promote you now?"

"Nope. I'm resigning this morning."

"What?"

"Yeah, I decided not to keep getting paid fry cook wages while serving as sous chef. I'm getting my old job back."

"At the store?"

"At the store. Let someone try to rob the cosmetics counter again. Go ahead—make my day," she said in her best Clint Eastwood voice.

"That's great news! Can't wait to see you again."

"When are you getting back?"

"That's a sore subject. Look, I have to run now. We'll talk soon."

Of course, Lena already knew about this. Tina had emailed her overnight. It had just slipped her mind with everything else going on. She asked me to leave the room so she could make a call. That triggered a name in the recesses of my mind—the mysterious Raleigh. I forgot to ask Tina about it. She probably knew who that was.

A few minutes later, Lena rushed out of the office. She told me she was heading back to the police station, and I might want to go with her. I certainly didn't but agreed to anyway.

We were kept waiting only 20 minutes before being ushered into DC Huntington's office. Lena laid out a printout of the tunnel map she had found and told him she would like to check out the basement of the building. Huntington said that was out of the question. The crime scene had been sealed and wasn't going to be reopened. Lena suggested that the perpetrator was living in the tunnels and would never be discovered unless they found his access door.

Huntington leaned back in his chair and gazed at Lena before answering. "Leave me that map. We'll look into it. The police are trained to do this sort of thing. You, young lady, need to stay as far away as possible. It's not safe. You might as well go back to the States."

Lena wasn't happy about that, I could tell. But something Huntington said triggered an iota of thought, a hint of a connection that I couldn't quite place. Little did I realize it was the beginning of the solution to the case.

27

Well, I guess that's that, I told Lena. We were officially off duty and could go home.

That's not that, she replied. There was a determined look on her face as we headed to the Tube station. A plot was forming in her head that would keep her on the job for a while longer. I didn't like it, but I'd seen that look before. Once Lena set her sights on a course, there was no steering her off the path.

When we got back to the apartment, Vi was there with the good news that she had found a couple of tickets for a flight leaving around midnight if we wanted her to book them. I was packed and ready to go. Lena said she couldn't leave yet.

"If you wanna go back, go on den," she said.

"What do you have to do? There's nothing you can do about the building anymore. It's over. The police won't let you in. It's dangerous anyway," I argued.

"You go on. I gotta figyah dis out." She headed back into the office. Vi raised her eyebrows at me, waiting for an answer. I could go, but I didn't feel right leaving Lena behind. There was also that little tug at my conscience telling me I was leaving the job half-done. But what more could I do?

I wrestled with this for a moment. Vi gave me an hour to make up my mind and left me alone to figure it out. I thought a cocktail might help but then decided against it for fear I would be caught in an endless loop. Plopping into a chair, I pondered. And pondered some more. Emmie figured prominently in my thought process. In the end, I just couldn't abandon Lena.

Peter, Paul and Mary had been warbling *Leaving on a jet plane...* in my head, but that was soon replaced with Frankie Valli crooning *Stay, just a little bit longer...*

141

Vi understood and said I could call her when we were ready to go. We had the run of the place until the next weekend, when she had another big party planned. Decorators and caterers would be arriving Friday to set up.

So we did have a deadline of sorts. Vi left, and I relayed it to Lena, who said she would scope things out in the next couple of days. She said to leave her alone—she was working on a plan of attack.

I was in a funk. Instead of resting comfortably in the cabin of a 747 as it prepared for takeoff, I was earthbound a while longer. It was time to get cheered up, and I knew just the person to do that.

"Hey, Emmie. You working?"

"Just sat down at my desk, Jim. You on the way home?"

"Well...not just yet. There's been another delay."

"Oh no!"

"Every time I think we're done here, something else crops up and we get pulled back in. But we have to vacate by Friday, so I'm going to see you next weekend come hell or high water."

"That would be nice," she said.

"Hey, I heard from Tina. She said she caught the robbers."

"Yes! Isn't that great? She spoke with Jane yesterday and gave her the news."

"A catcher. Wearing nail polish."

"Beg pardon?"

"The guy with the fingernail polish. He was a catcher trying out for the Saint Paul Saints. Tina didn't give you the details?"

"No, just that the robbers were in custody."

"Anyway, that's half the good news. The other half is that Tina is coming back to the store."

"To work?"

"Yeah, she said she applied for her old job."

"Really? That's news to me."

"Can you check the new hires file? See when she starts?"

"I'll check, but you know there's a hiring freeze on right now."

"What?"

"Mr. Foster put that in place last week. I didn't catch all the details."

"Well, Tina sounded like it was a done deal."

"I'll look into it. Did you hear about your replacement?"

"The guy from Vegas?"

"Right. He's disappeared. Or at least no one can locate him. He was supposed to meet with the fire inspectors Friday. Something about false alarms being reported last week. He didn't show up. Jane had to meet with them because Bambi had no clue where he was."

"They tried his number?"

"And the hotel he's staying at. No sign of him over the weekend. The maids said the room was still straight from when they last made it up."

"So someone was setting off false alarms?"

"No, Jim. Well, they weren't sure. They suspected that the alarm in the basement was shorted out. At least they couldn't tell that it had been triggered."

"All the more reason for me to get back there ASAP," I said.

"I know. I miss you so much," she said in that heart-melting voice.

After a few more private moments, I hung up and sought out Lena. She was still at the computer and sketching some sort of map. I sat on the chair next to the desk in silence and gave her a few minutes to complete what she was working on.

When she stopped drawing and smiled, I knew she had a plan. What she outlined for me sounded like one of Freddie's harebrained schemes.

And I knew I would go along with it.

28

Working alongside Lena for days on end was a stressful experience. Although I had been working with Lena and Tina for three years, I really didn't see that much of them in the store on a daily basis. And I certainly didn't know much about their lives outside of La Scala. I was missing the 90 percent of the iceberg below the water.

For example, it was only by fluke chance that I discovered one of Lena's hidden talents—juggling.

While I was standing by the cosmetics counter one day chatting with Tina, Lena happened to walk by just as my cellphone rang. As I was reaching for it, I accidentally knocked a nail polish tester bottle off the counter.

Before it could hit the floor, Lena snatched it out of mid-air. She then proceeded to pick up three more bottles of polish and juggle them, occasionally flipping one behind her back. This went on for seemingly hours but was probably only a minute. Tina and I stood in awe and too stunned to speak.

Finally, Lena caught all four bottles in one hand, placed them back in a row on the counter and casually walked off without saying a word. We watched her leave, then Tina exclaimed, "What was *that?!*"

Not content to let such an exhibition go unexplained, Tina and I plied Lena with drinks at The Crater one evening and dragged the story out of her: It seems she got her start as an entertainer at an early age. Her mother took her to a circus show in Lafayette, Louisiana, when she was eight. The juggler rode a unicycle while keeping a number of eggs aloft. When one eluded his grasp and fell on the ground, it didn't break—it bounced. Rubber eggs.

"I could do dat wit' *real* eggs," Lena declared. She found a book at the library and studied and practiced until she could keep five balls aloft in varying formations, with an occasional flip behind her back. She won her grammar school talent contest by juggling coffee mugs and golf balls, ending by catching the balls in the mugs.

"Thought about joinin' da circus," she said, "but da freaks creeped me out." After high school, she worked as a magician's apprentice for a bit before deciding there weren't many career paths for jugglers. She admitted she hadn't tossed up anything in years until the nail polish incident.

"You could earn some change pulling that trick out in bars," I suggested.

"Do I hang out in baws, Beers?" she replied.

"You're in one right now," Tina countered.

"Not fa long," Lena replied, polishing off her drink and quickly departing.

Tina likewise was an enigma. I was fairly certain she was a tomboy growing up, based on her dress and mannerisms. But Tina also had a hidden side that only revealed itself by accident one evening when I was carousing with Freddie. We wandered into an unfamiliar bar not far from the Metrodome. We had just watched the Twins get flattened by the Yankees, a not unexpected outcome.

A honky-tonk band was playing on a small stage a stone's throw from the bar, where we managed to acquire a couple of longnecks. The female singer was belting out "Walkin' After Midnight" by Patsy Cline. It was not my favorite genre, but the girl had a fantastic voice that hit every note perfectly.

When I approached the bandstand to get a closer look, I almost dropped my bottle. The singer was Tina, wearing lots of makeup and a blond wig, and dressed in a stunning blue lamé number that accentuated her curves—very out of character for her. She didn't see me gawking at her probably because the stage lights prevented her from making out faces. But she was startled when Freddie came up beside me and yelled, "Hey, Tina! Looking good!"

At the end of her number, the band took a break and she went backstage. We waited, and when the band re-emerged, no Tina. The guitar player sang lead for the next few songs. I asked at the bar when the girl singer would return, and the barkeep said that was the end of her set.

I asked Tina about it the next time I saw her at work. She told me she didn't want to talk about it. Lena knew the scoop, however. Tina was a local phenom in high school, where she regularly starred in musicals. This was in a small town in the northwest part of the state.

When she arrived in the Twin Cities for college, Tina hooked up with the theater crowd and landed roles in small productions. But she had visions of eventually getting to Broadway and becoming a star.

She even signed with an agent and thought she had a good shot at a role in an off-Broadway revival of "Annie Get Your Gun." She was packed and ready to board a flight, Lena reported, when she got a call from the agent saying the role went to another singer. Turned out the other singer was a bimbo shacking up with said agent, whom Tina summarily fired.

Disillusioned, she concentrated on her criminal justice studies but grew tired of the school grind. A grunge bassist had seen her in one of her roles and approached her about joining his band. Lacking any other profitable options, she accepted and became her singing persona: Lynda Mansell, named for the main character in a movie she enjoyed called "Wish You Were Here."

Apparently, that didn't last long but she enjoyed the bright lights of minor stardom. When the same bassist approached her recently about resurrecting her singing career in a new group, she was willing—on the condition that her real name would never be used.

Lena said if anyone ever found out she was moonlighting as a crooner—excluding Lena, of course—she would have to move to another city. No explanation was given, so I never pressed the issue. Lena only told me the back story after I had discovered Tina's secret. She swore me to silence. Tina will retain her anonymous stardom.

But I have managed to watch her from the shadows a couple of times and been very impressed. She could go places, but she doesn't want to. Sort of the opposite of me. I want to go places but can't.

If only life were fair.

29

Monday, April 16

Bright and early, we were sitting in a coffee shop across Knightsbridge from the warehouse. Lena was giving me orders and going over the details of her plan. Communication was vital to the mission, she said, so she had stopped at a cheapo electronics store and acquired a prepaid cellphone called GoTalk. I rang it to make sure it worked. She was also carrying a compass. I jokingly offered to buy her some bread crumbs so she could find her way back, but she didn't think that was funny.

She finished her coffee and scooted out. Watching her cross the street, I couldn't help thinking about those old TV series featuring female detectives. She was dressed sort of like Catwoman, black long-sleeve top and tights. Several passing men did double takes as she made her way down the sidewalk. Inconspicuous, she wasn't.

The waitress kept coming by to see if I wanted anything else, and after about six cups of coffee I decided I'd better eat something. She brought a waffle the size of a pizza pan, and I began to slowly work my way through it. Lena called once to say she had found her way in a few blocks behind the warehouse. It was really dirty and smelly in there, she said.

If I had been thinking clearly, I probably would have realized that at some point her cell signal would crap out, and she would be all alone in the catacombs. Perhaps in mortal danger. But again, this was Lena's show and, based on her normal level-headedness, I felt she knew what she was doing.

The waffle became a part of history and no more news from Lena. I had just about decided to bolt across the street and break into the building when I saw something. It looked like a flash of light coming from the interior of the warehouse. It briefly streaked across the front picture window. It could have been a reflection of something on the exterior, a headlight on a turning car. It was an overcast and gloomy day, after all. But I thought I'd better give Lena a call to see if that was her on the inside.

No answer. She might not be in a position to talk. I decided on the only course of action available—wait for something to happen.

My attention was riveted on the front window across the way when my phone rang and caused me to jump.

"Are you inside?" I asked.

"Inside? What are you talking about?" Joe T answered.

"Oh, hi, Joe T. I thought you were Lena."

"No, I'm not. Where are you?"

"In a coffee shop across the street from the warehouse," I said. "We're on a little reconnaissance mission. Lena is trying to find a way in—"

"There have been two murders there, maybe more, and you sent Lena in alone? For fuck's sake!"

"I didn't want her to go but—"

"Get your ass outta there and get back to the apartment."

"But Lena—"

"No buts. Do it now." He hung up. I didn't get a chance to ask him why, or what was waiting for us there. Maybe those plane tickets? Vi had probably booked the midnight flight, and we had to go. Lena would have to give up her quest.

I rang her again. Still no answer. This was worrisome. She said she would touch base at regular intervals, so she must have no phone signal. Or maybe something happened to her. The thought suddenly terrorized me, and I bolted out of the shop without paying the bill. Somehow I made it across the road without getting run over. I peeked in the front window.

Part of the first floor was visible through the murky light coming in the front windows. My eyes must have been playing tricks on me because I thought I saw a flicker of a shadow moving in the interior. Since I had no clue where Lena had entered the subterranean chambers, there was little I could do but keep trying to call her.

When I looked up, the waitress was standing next to me with a scowl, holding out the bill. After my profuse apologies and a generous tip, she traipsed back across the street, and I resumed my unhidden stakeout.

"Whatcha see in dere?" The voice startled me. I turned to find Lena beside me, also peering into the warehouse.

"Lena! You're safe, thank God! Why didn't you call?"

"No signal. Also couldn't find a way in dere. If da perp got in through da tunnels, he musta had a key. Or maybe it's one a doze Eloi."

"Eloi?"

"You know. 'Time Machine'? Evah seen dat movie?"

"We need to just drop all this, I think. The police have the building sealed up, so if we do get in there, we're going to be arrested. Besides, it's too dangerous."

"Yeah. Mebbe you right."

We headed to the Tube, and I convinced Lena that it was time for her to pack up and go back home with me. There was nothing more we could do. Our assignment would have to remain incomplete, thwarted by forces beyond our control.

Once again, I turned out to be wrong in my estimation of our imminent departure. When we closed the door to the apartment, I heard a voice call from somewhere, "Vi? Is that you?"

"Someone's heah," Lena observed.

I gave her a no-shit look before heading toward where I thought the sound was coming from—the kitchen in the north wing.

"It's not Vi," I called. "Jim Biersovich and Lena Fangeaux." As I approached the kitchen, a smiling head popped around the corner.

"Mr. Biersovich! So good to see you!"

I almost wet my pants, and I heard Lena gasp behind me.

"Mr. Scalabrino! What are you doing here?" I asked.

He laughed. "Call me Johnny," he said. He beckoned us into the kitchen, where he had sandwich fixings spread out on the island and was assembling what I assumed would be a Dagwood.

"You hungry? Plenty here," he said, motioning toward the array of meats, cheeses, breads and condiments.

"We could eat," Lena replied, heading to the sink to wash up.

"You look like a cat burglar," Scalabrino said with a smile.

"We've been out on a little reconnaissance of the building, sir...Johnny," I said.

"Yeah, undah da pawkin' garage tree blocks ovah," Lena added. "Couldn't find a way in, though." She started layering cheese and meat on a slice of bread.

"So, Johnny...why are you in London? We were just about to head back and give you the full report," I said. I noticed he wasn't wearing his usual more formal attire. He had on deck shoes, gray slacks and a white polo shirt, like he had been out strolling in the park.

"Mr. Biersovich—"

"Call me Jim."

"Your mission may be done. Then again, I may need you a bit longer. Vi has been keeping me up to date with some things going on that I needed to attend to personally. And this transaction seems to have hit a snag."

"I'll say."

"Coupla snags, also known as murdah," Lena threw in.

"I'd like to visit the owners," he said.

"The Featherstonaughs."

"Precisely. I need to determine once and for all if this purchase is in any way possible. I'm getting mixed signals."

"We've been getting those ever since we've been here," I said. "The snag isn't the Featherstonaughs, though. It's Jasmine Sloane. That's Stony Perkins' wife. Stony is the sibling who died...murdered. He apparently didn't want to sell for some reason. We've been trying to figure out why, but he can't tell us, the other siblings don't know and Jasmine is hospitalized, so she's no help either."

"Who's the attorney for the estate?"

"Beaton Dobbs. Well, he's Jasmine's lawyer. He's no help either."

"I'd like to speak personally with this Miss Sloane. Perhaps I can convince her it's in her interest to sell."

"Good luck wit' dat," Lena said.

"Would you ride up to Luton with me, Mr. Biersovich?" Scalabrino asked.

"But sir, we're supposed to be flying out any time now. In fact, I'm just waiting for Vi to call—"

That's when I heard the front door slam and footsteps heading our way. Needless to say, we got another surprise when Vi walked through the kitchen door, followed closely by Joe T.

But the biggest shock came when Vi walked right up to Scalabrino and planted a kiss square on the lips. "Hello, love," she said.

Lena and I exchanged stunned looks. My head was spinning, and I supposed Lena's was also because neither of us said anything. We just stood there, watching with stupid expressions.

"Jim, Lena," Vi said.

"How's it going?" Joe T asked, then dug into the smorgasbord. "Man, I'm famished!"

Still too bewildered to speak, I stood mute, waiting for an explanation. Scalabrino leaned against a counter and took a big bite out of his sandwich, smiling at me.

Vi began reciting a checklist of activities: "I have the cleaners coming in Wednesday. At two tomorrow you go for your fitting. After that, you should get a little trim. Looking a little shaggy around the edges. Friday the caterers are doing a walk-through. They have some new folks who haven't been here before, but I don't suspect there will be a problem. Then Saturday the decorators arrive at eleven so we need to be out of the way. I've reserved a table at the chateau for lunch. You can make that, I trust. Then back here for six for the final setup. Oh, I need to call that nail salon. Excuse me, all." Then she exited.

"Busy girl," Joe T observed between bites.

Scalabrino nodded and continued devouring his lunch.

Vi had skedaddled before I could inquire about our flight schedule. But somehow I sensed that was delayed yet again.

"Ya got a big pawty, I heah," Lena said.

"Quite so," Scalabrino replied.

Then I heard the door slam once more and a shout of "Yo, Beers!" which meant more trouble was approaching.

30

Freddie entered the kitchen, and his big grin immediately fell when he saw Scalabrino and Joe T.

"You remember Freddie," I said to Joe T. "Mr. Scalabrino, this is Fred Skelton. Works for the Herald. Sportswriter." Scalabrino just nodded and continued munching.

"Wh-what's going on here?" Freddie asked, looking back and forth between the kitchen team.

"Pawty plannin'," Lena said, as she finished off her sandwich.

"What are you doing here, Mr. Skelton?" Scalabrino asked.

"Well, sir, I came here to interview my uncle, Sir Reginald Skelton. It sort of fell through, though."

"Is that so?" Scalabrino replied. "I know Reggie. Loose cannon, as I recall. Leaps without a net."

"That's him all right," Freddie replied.

"So now you're just what—hanging out?" Scalabrino asked. Freddie nodded.

"Have some lunch, Mr. Skelton. Joseph, come with me." He led Joe T out of the kitchen. Freddie looked at me, shrugged and headed to the spread.

"What's that under your arm?" I asked, pointing to a thin square bag.

"Oh," Freddie said. "Here ya go." He handed it to me. I opened the bag and removed an album. It was the first Molly Hatchet record, one I didn't have in my collection.

"Thanks, Freddie. Where did you get this?"

"Hick gave it to me to pass along to you. Something about a reward. Anyway, I think I got a good story. Turns out he was one of the promoters who brought Prince to London in '86. So I got a local angle. That should keep my editors at bay."

"But you're a sportswriter," I argued. He ate while I examined the goods. The label said it was a demo copy of the first album. The record itself looked to be pristine, while the sleeve was signed by all the band members. There was even a crude drawing of a hatchet, presumably done by one of the players. While it wasn't my main musical interest, the rarity of the item ensured that it would be a nice addition to my rock collection.

"How did you even get Hick to see you?" I asked.

"I'm very persuasive when I need to be," he said.

Scalabrino returned and told me to get ready—we were going for a ride. Joe T pulled Freddie aside and asked him what his plans were for the remainder of the day. Likewise with Lena. I didn't catch all of their conversation—something about an assignment—because Scalabrino ordered me to go put on some "sensible shoes."

When I returned to the kitchen in my sneakers, it was vacant and the food was put away. Scalabrino strolled in and I almost didn't recognize him. In place of the leisure wear he had on earlier, he was in a black warmup suit, high-top sneakers and a riding cap. He looked like Jackie Gleason in "The Honeymooners." It was a startling transformation. Instead of his usual rich, eccentric businessman look, Scalabrino had become a normal shlub. Like me.

He led me out and down the stairs to the curb, where a black cab was waiting. As I opened the back door to enter, Scalabrino got in front and said, "To the baron's, Billy."

"Right, gov'nah," the cabbie answered, and we were off. He looked familiar and it took a while to place him. He was the cab driver who delivered us to the apartment initially. Obviously on the payroll.

A couple of times I asked Scalabrino where we were going, but he just smiled and said I would find out soon.

Soon turned out to be later than I reckoned. We headed north and left London. About 20 minutes into the ride I realized we were on the way to Luton. OK, I thought. Carrying coals to Newcastle. So be it. It's his show, I reasoned, I'm just along for the ride.

We pulled up in front of the Featherstonaugh estate behind the Bentley, which Marston was polishing. He glanced at us with a sort of sneer and resumed his buffing.

Scalabrino sprang out of the cab and marched to the front door, with me tagging along. He hadn't explained his approach or what I was even there for, but I surmised it was to speak when spoken to and take notes.

When a butler answered the door, Scalabrino announced himself and his intention to speak with the baron. The butler let us into the foyer and asked us to remain while he found Baron Featherstonaugh, who was apparently playing croquet on the west lawn. Off he went, and Scalabrino surveyed his surroundings. "Nice digs," he commented.

After a few minutes, John Featherstonaugh arrived and introduced himself to Scalabrino, nodding at me.

"Baron, I'm Johnny Scalabrino," the boss began. "You can call me Johnny."

"And you can call me John," Featherstonaugh replied. "We usually dispense with the pretense of peerage." He smiled and invited us into the den, where we got comfortable.

"The reason for our visit is I'd like to get the lay of the land regarding your warehouse," Scalabrino said. Featherstonaugh nodded, closing his eyes. "My associate, Mr. Biersovich"—he waved a hand toward me—"has been my emissary here in an effort to gauge the efficacy of the property. But I felt it was time to get serious about this and try to wrap things up."

"I understand perfectly, Johnny," he replied. "However, I'm afraid you'll need to seek redress elsewhere. You see, my siblings and I are perfectly willing to sell, but things have been..." He searched for the right word. "...complicated."

"By your brother's untimely demise," Scalabrino offered.

"Precisely. My *half*-brother's...wife...Jasmine Sloane, holds all the cards now. While we would like to divest, she has dug her heels in and for some inexplicable reason won't play ball."

"Half-brother?"

"Stony was somewhat younger than Jimmy, Bitsy and me. He came along after our father died and my mother had remarried. He is...was of another generation and only half of a blood relative. And of course he ran in different circles, a lifestyle far removed from the Featherstonaughs, I might add."

"Is it a question of money?" Scalabrino asked.

Featherstonaugh shook his head. "No, no, no. I'm afraid it's more than that. But exactly what I can't say. Stony often resisted the aims of the trust. In this instance, he must have undertaken some tilting at windmills notion, and Miss Sloane has been unavailable to confer with."

"I see. Well, we won't take up any more of your time," Scalabrino said, rising. "Thank you, John. We'll see ourselves out."

Back in the cab, Scalabrino sat beside me in back. "Where does Miss Sloane live?" he asked.

"She's hospitalized right now," I said. "Not having visitors."

"We'll see about that. Tell Billy how to get there."

Along the way, I described Jasmine and her overprotective lawyer. Getting the real story on her reluctance to sell was another matter. I told him how Stony had read something in his mother's diary that convinced him he needed to hold onto the building. But Jasmine couldn't locate the diary. Also the mysterious key marked with a G.

Why a G? he asked. No clue, I answered.

Scalabrino nodded and I could see the gears turning in his head. He also asked what was the story with the chauffeur. Probably the killer, I replied, only half-joking.

Joe T rang Scalabrino's mobile phone during the ride, and I only caught "good, good," "excellent" and "keep me posted" from his end of the conversation.

We arrived at the Luton and Dunstable Hospital, and Scalabrino passed himself off as Jasmine's American uncle who was concerned about her condition. Despite the nurse's contention that she wasn't seeing visitors, Scalabrino talked her into at least letting us peek in her room to find out whether she would see us.

As the door cracked open, I could see Beany Dobbs standing by the bedside. He looked up and headed us off before we could enter.

"Miss Sloane can't have visitors," Dobbs said after forcing us back into the hallway and closing the door.

"This is Mr. Scalabrino," I said.

"I've come all the way from America to see Miss Sloane," he explained. "I'm eager to buy the warehouse building and I need to know—"

"That's out of the question," Dobbs interrupted. "Miss Sloane is in no condition to make such a decision right now."

"What is her condition?" Scalabrino asked.

"She's suffering from depression and acute anxiety. You see, her husband was recently murdered," Dobbs said.

"I know about that," Scalabrino answered. "Surely Miss Sloane doesn't need the headache of managing a vacant property on top of all that. I'm willing to offer a good price for the building."

Dobbs narrowed his eyes. "I'm not sure you understand the gravity of the situation, Mr. ...Scalabrino, is it? Jasmine's husband is dead. Gone. She has no one now. She is in pain. This is the last thing she needs to worry about. Now, good day!" He turned and re-entered the room, closing the door with force.

Scalabrino stood a minute staring at the closed door, then said, "I don't like him."

"He is a bit of a dick," I said.

"And I don't trust the bastard."

"That too."

He instructed me to head back to the cab and wait for him. Fifteen minutes later he strolled out, got in the front and told Billy to drive. Scalabrino asked for Jasmine's address. And he wanted me to list everyone else I had encountered in Luton, so I told him about the Irish wake with Stony's friends.

We pulled up in front of Jasmine's cottage and got out. Scalabrino poked his head in the driver's side window, said something to Billy and off he drove.

Over my objections and concern about Scalabrino's intentions, we approached the house. He knocked.

"Sir, if Jasmine's in the hospital—"

My comment was interrupted by the door opening. Mrs. Trimble, the neighbor, gazed at us and said curtly, "No solicitors, thank you," and started to close the door.

"Mrs. Trimble," I replied. That stopped her. "Hi. I was here before to see Jasmine. Jim Biersovich. And this is Mr. Scalabrino."

"Might we come in for a moment?" Scalabrino asked with a warm smile.

"Jasmine is in hospital," she said.

"Yes, we're quite aware," Scalabrino replied. "This will only take a minute. If you would be so kind."

She had a worried look on her face but stepped aside to let us pass through.

We were standing in the living room when Mrs. Trimble asked, "What's all this then?"

"We won't take up much of your time," Scalabrino began. "We just have a couple of questions that we can't seem to get answered due to Jasmine's...condition."

"Well, I don't know how I can help," she replied. She wrung her hands a bit, then invited us to sit. "I was just going to have a cuppa. Would you like some?"

"That would be delightful," Scalabrino answered.

"Won't be a mo," she said, and scooted into the kitchen.

"What's the plan?" I whispered.

"Find the diary and that key," he said.

"She's not going to just let us search the place."

"You'll think of something," he said.

31

While Mrs. Trimble was assembling the teacups and scones, I tiptoed around the room and looked in all the obvious spots but saw nothing resembling a diary or a strange G key.

As I heard the tinkle of china, I curtailed my inspection and rejoined Scalabrino on the couch. Mrs. Trimble served tea and was nibbling on a scone when Scalabrino began.

"Mrs. Trimble, I've come from America to buy some property that Miss Sloane owns. Actually, jointly owns with her late husband's siblings. Mr. Biersovich was here a few days ago to speak with Miss Sloane on my behalf. And that's why we're here." He took a sip of tea and looked toward me. That was my cue to invent a story. It only took a few seconds, amazingly.

"That's right," I said. "Mr. Scalabrino sent me here to negotiate a deal, and when I was speaking with Jasmine...Miss Sloane...about the particulars, she wanted to see the offer in black and white. So I had a document prepared that showed the financial terms and also included some proprietary information that would be very detrimental to Mr. Scalabrino's business if we don't get that document back. Miss Sloane was going to look it over and get back to me, and now she's unavailable."

Scalabrino smiled and took over the narrative. "So you see, we're here to acquire that document. Since Miss Sloane doesn't intend to sell, the document is useless to her. But it's still very important to me. If it fell into the wrong hands..." He let those ominous words sink in. Mrs. Trimble nodded with a concerned look.

"Well, I've been keeping her place tidy while she's down, and I haven't come across anything like that. Perhaps she gave it to her solicitor?"

The little misdirection was growing into a big fat lie, but no turning back now. "Mr. Dobbs didn't know anything about it when I asked him. Jasmine said she was going to tuck it into a book for safekeeping," I offered. "Would you mind if I looked for it?"

"I don't know...," she said.

"Mrs. Trimble, this piece of paper could ruin me." Scalabrino gave her the most hangdog look I'd ever seen. "And I'm offering a reward to anyone who assists in its recovery." He made a great show of taking his wallet out and opening it to reveal a wad of pounds. That was the clincher. Mrs. Trimble was suitably impressed and jumped up to help.

"This shelf has most of her books," she pointed out. "And I believe there are some in the study."

"Perhaps if we split up and each took a room," Scalabrino suggested.

"Oh, yes," she replied. "Very well then." She exited to the study. Scalabrino pointed me to the bedroom, and he headed to the kitchen.

The nightstand next to Jasmine's neatly made bed held a single volume, a Jackie Collins novel. Nothing of note under the bed or in the closet. The hall linen closet was equally devoid of anything useful. I made one more pass through the living room, but nothing turned up.

We reassembled there and Mrs. Trimble reported she had found nothing of the sort we were seeking. Scalabrino inquired about the garage. She was skeptical but led him out there. I was left to scour the rest of the interior.

As Mrs. Trimble reported, there was nothing in the study of note, not even a computer. A half-assembled boat in a bottle sat on a desk in the corner. The drawers contained glues, tools and paint, but no journal or key marked with a G. The tiny bathroom had a couple of magazines and the usual assortment of hygiene products. I did note the presence of several prescriptions in the cabinet, including Percocet and Zyprexa. I was pretty sure what the former was intended to treat but had no idea about the latter.

Just as I was about to give up the quest, I spotted a hatch in the hall ceiling. The attic! Dragging a chair from the living room, I stood on it and pulled the small ring attached to the hatch. It sprang down to reveal a folding ladder. Up I went into a nest of cobwebs, which enveloped my head like a hair net. Waving my arms wildly, I cleared some breathing room and peered in all directions. It was almost pitch black, but there were some small glimmers of light at the far edges, presumably at the locations of vents in the eaves.

It was too dark to see anything except the immediate 2 inches surrounding me, and I lacked a flashlight. After a few minutes of examining the attic, I concluded that the thickness of the dust around the hatch and its uniformity indicated I was the only one who had been up here in years.

Scalabrino soon returned from the garage with Mrs. Trimble in his wake. "Nothing," he said to me. Then to her: "Thank you for your time, Mrs. Trimble. We won't keep you any longer." He turned and walked toward the front door.

"If I come across that paper, I can ring you," she said. "'Course, Mr. Perkins' friend may have picked it up by mistake."

That stopped Scalabrino in his tracks and he turned. "Perkins?" he asked.

"Stony," I said. "His real name is...*was* Samuel Perkins."

"Which friend of Mr. Perkins are you speaking about, Mrs. Trimble?" he asked.

"It was the gentleman Mr. Perkins used to work for. Oh dear, I've forgotten his name."

"Enthoven?" I offered.

"Yes, that's it. He came round yesterday. Said he had Mr. Perkins' last pay. Insisted I put it in a safe place." She hesitated before saying, "It's in the other teakettle."

I could see gears grinding in Scalabrino's brain, but he made no further comment, just turned and exited. I followed.

Billy was back and waiting at the curb. Scalabrino leaned in the front window and whispered something to Billy, then told me we needed to pay a visit to this Enthoven fellow. I guessed he might be at the pub if he wasn't on a jobsite. On the way there, Scalabrino opined that Enthoven had snatched the diary when Mrs. Trimble was fiddling in the kitchen. Possible, I admitted.

Billy dropped us at the sidewalk and zoomed off. Inside the pub, business was slow, and I saw no sign of the landscaper. The barkeep hadn't seen him. Scalabrino revealed that he was looking to redo his gardens at his estate and needed to get in touch with Enthoven. The bartender said he might have his mobile number and went into a back room. A minute later, he returned with a number on a torn sheet of paper and said Scalabrino should say Cobbie sent him, so he would get the discount. So Cobbie would get a finder's fee, I translated.

I dialed, got Enthoven on the line and related the current story. He seemed quite interested and said he was just finishing up some sod work down the road from the pub. He would meet us there within the half-hour.

Scalabrino found a corner table and suggested I acquire some drinks while we waited. He wanted a gimlet but was afraid of how it would be presented in the current surroundings, so he settled for vodka rocks. I ordered a black and tan.

Time passed, our drinks elapsed, and I was dispatched for another round. Billy came in, whispered something to Scalabrino, then got a nod and left again. Finally, 45 minutes and another round later, Enthoven showed up and arrived at our table grinning.

"Sorry about that, chaps. Work ran long."

"No worries, Mr. Enthoven." Scalabrino extended his hand, introduced himself, then quickly got to the point, inquiring as to whether Enthoven had removed anything from Stony's house.

"No, sir. I just brought his final check." He had an abject look. "Terrible business about Stony. I hope they catch the knobs what did him in."

Scalabrino signaled the barkeep for another round, got one for Enthoven and began his line of questioning. Did he have any idea about who would kill Stony? Did Stony have any enemies? Was there something Stony told him about the warehouse building? And so on.

Enthoven could offer no assistance and after polishing off his beer, excused himself, saying he had another site to visit.

"Unfortunately, he's telling the truth," Scalabrino said after he left.

"How can you tell?"

"Mr. Biersovich, when you've been in business as long as I have, and dealt with unscrupulous people on a daily basis, you know when someone is creating an invention."

"So what next?"

He didn't respond, just pulled out his phone and dialed.

"Hello, Joseph...No, nothing on this end...I see...Yes, just a couple more to look into...Let's reconvene at..." He glanced at his watch, a diamond-studded Rolex. "...6 o'clock. We'll lay out the agenda then...Yes, I know." He hung up and said, "Let's go."

Following him out the door, I saw no sign of the taxi. He stood on the sidewalk with his arms folded, staring into the distance in obviously deep contemplation. I waited silently, for lack of anything better to do.

In ten minutes, Billy showed up and we hopped in the taxi. Scalabrino grunted and off we went, back down to London.

So many questions were flowing through my head I didn't know where to start. But there was one thing that was plaguing me the most.

"About Vi," I began.

Scalabrino glanced over at me and smirked. "She is a rare gem indeed," he said, but offered no further explanation of her role in his organization. But I suspected high-end call girl might be on her curriculum vitae.

Lena, Freddie and Joe T were eating pizza in the dining room when we arrived. The savory aroma of pepperoni, anchovies and banana peppers made me salivate, and I quickly joined them at the table.

"Report," Scalabrino said from his post at the far end of the table. Joe T began a litany of their activities. Freddie visited the police station on the pretense of doing a story on Samuel "Stony" Perkins and his untimely demise. Lena did research on the Featherstonaugh clan, while Joe T staked out the warehouse building to watch for intruders. They had little useful information to offer.

Then Scalabrino recounted our undertakings and laid out the next day's schedule: All hands on deck in Luton for a full-court press on the likely suspects, along with the continued quest for the elusive diary and a curious key.

After dinner I called Emmie. She was consternated, I could tell. She didn't understand why we were still in London if the assignment was doomed to fail. I could offer little explanation. I detected a note of unease in her voice, but she didn't want to get into it over the phone.

I slept restlessly, with a knot of congealed pizza in my gut, dreaming of airplanes waiting to take me to far-away places.

Typically, I was running for a flight but arrived too late to board. It had already left the gate.

32

Tuesday, April 17

As I was pouring a second cup of coffee, I heard the apartment door open and close. Joe T walked into the kitchen where Lena, Scalabrino and I were breakfasting.

"All done?" Scalabrino asked.

Joe T nodded.

"Good. OK, folks, let's get ready to leave in 30 minutes. Mr. Biersovich, please make sure your friend is up."

I hadn't seen a sign of Freddie, so I went to the bedroom he had last inhabited. He wasn't there. After a short search, I found him in the office, tapping away on the computer.

"Freddie, you need to get ready to go—"

"I'm all set, Beers. Just looking up one thing here...aha...as I thought." He turned and beamed at me. "This is going to be fun."

Freddie's idea of fun usually meant trouble for me, but this was Scalabrino's show, so I didn't have a choice if I wanted to eventually return home. And oddly, Freddie seemed like he was engaged in the mission, way out of character for him. Could he be changing? And maturing? I had my doubts.

Waiting at the curb was a stretch limo. The full cast was assembled: Scalabrino, Joe T, Lena, Freddie, me, Billy, Vi, plus a couple of guys and a woman I hadn't seen before. We piled into the limo and set off, with Scalabrino holding court. He was in his normal attire, an expensive suit, and was holding his proverbial prop, a putter.

"Here's what we're going to do," he began. "Vi, you're at the hospital. I want reports on anyone who goes in and out of Jasmine's room. Especially that lawyer, what's-his-name."

"Beany?" I offered.

"Right. Joe T, you take his office. Harold—" He indicated one of the new guys in the group. "You're at Jasmine's home. No one goes in or out, even Mrs. Trimble." He provided a brief description.

"Mr. Skelton." Freddie perked up at mention of his name. "Stake out the bar. Make the rounds. Get any intelligence you can on Stony and his last days. Miss Fangeaux, visit the sister." He snapped his fingers a couple of times.

"Bitsy," I said.

"Bitsy. Go visit her, grill her in any way you can. See what she knows about the diary, if anything. Colin, you're on the brother, James. Billy will be on call for pickup. Here's the number." Scalabrino recited it. "Sally, police records. Mr. Biersovich, you're with me."

Joe T gave a brief rundown of his secret early morning mission, setting up video cameras to capture signs of intrusion at the Featherstonaugh warehouse. Two more of Scalabrino's men were on stakeout there.

The rest of the ride up to Luton was silent, with everyone contemplating their assignments. I didn't really want to do this, but like the Beatles refrain, *I'm gonna try with a little help from my friends.*

One by one, passengers were dropped off at their posts, until only Scalabrino and I were left in the limo, along with Billy at the wheel. We rode up to the front of the Featherstonaugh mansion and parked in the circular drive behind the Bentley. No sign of Marston.

Since the boss hadn't spelled out exactly what new tactic we were going to employ, I was once again unsure of my role but by this time had learned to follow his lead. The diary was the vital element, he believed, and we were going to do anything we could to find it. Locating the mystery key would be a bonus.

As far as I knew, we were arriving unannounced. It was late morning, but there was no sign of life as we approached the front door. I used the lion's-head knocker, and we waited. No sound of shuffling feet came from the void beyond the door.

I was about to opine that no one was home when the baron came around the far side of the manor and approached the front steps.

"Good morning, gents," he said with a stern look. "I didn't know you were coming."

"It's an impromptu visit," Scalabrino replied. "A matter of urgency, I'm afraid." He answered with his own grim expression.

John Featherstonaugh showed us in, led us to the kitchen and offered tea. Scalabrino declined and indicated he would like to get right to the point and not waste any of his time. We sat at the small table in the alcove.

"We are on a quest for a document that has critical importance to both of our stated intentions."

Featherstonaugh looked puzzled. "What would that be?" he asked.

"The sale of the property on Knightsbridge," Scalabrino answered.

"Ah, yes." Featherstonaugh nodded and grimaced. "But you understand the situation we're in."

"I do," Scalabrino said. "But there could be a way to resolve the impasse."

At that point, the cook entered the kitchen carrying a box. He placed it on the preparation table near the sink and began removing items: a pair of ducks, some spices and a gleaming new cleaver with price tag still attached.

"I'll need to begin preparations soon, sir," he said.

"Quite so, Ridley. We won't be a moment," Featherstonaugh answered. The cook left. "So, exactly how do you propose to solve the situation?"

"We need to find that document," Scalabrino replied.

"What sort of document?"

"A diary."

Featherstonaugh was puzzled. "Diary? Whose diary?"

"Your mother's diary," Scalabrino said. "It was in the possession of your half-brother. Miss Sloane told Mr. Biersovich that Stony wanted to hold onto the property because of something in that diary."

"Preposterous!" Featherstonaugh blurted.

"No, this is quite serious," Scalabrino said. "In fact, so serious that two people have been murdered to protect the secret contained in that diary."

Featherstonaugh was speechless. He stared at Scalabrino for a minute, glanced at me, then looked out the window to the side garden. When he turned back, there was a look of dread on his face. "Are you suggesting that...that I..."

"Not at all," Scalabrino said. "But if you know something, you need to tell us, unless you want to get the local authorities involved."

"I don't know anything about a diary and I certainly know nothing about the murders," Featherstonaugh replied indignantly. "I think you should leave now." He rose and stepped aside for us to pass. We took the cue and left.

Outside, Marston was sitting on a bench in the front garden, eyeing us as we re-entered the limo.

"Billy, did you speak with that gentleman over there?" Scalabrino asked.

"Yeah, boss. A right nutter, that one. Asked me if I had spent time in the nick."

"Find out about him."

"Will do, sir."

"Anyone report in?"

"Vi said she went to the hospital room Miss Sloane had occupied but she wasn't there anymore. She's trying to find out where she was moved. Joe T found a safe in the solicitor's office but didn't want to break in without a go-ahead. The young lady with the accent..."

"Lena," I offered.

"She didn't find the sister at home. Spoke with the husband. That's it."

Scalabrino closed his eyes and folded his hands over his midsection. I waited. Billy fidgeted with the rear-view mirror. After a moment, Scalabrino opened his eyes and said, "Hospital." We headed off.

Vi was standing at the curb as we rolled up, then popped in the back next to Scalabrino.

"Something called St. Andrew's Cottage in Dunstable," she said. "Psychiatric care. Medium security. I suppose we'll need a ruse."

Scalabrino considered that, then said, "Perhaps. Suggestion?"

"Billy, you still have that kit?" she asked.

"Yes, mum."

"You might want to pull over somewhere. We're going to need it."

33

The "kit" turned out to be a fake ID machine. Billy took Vi's picture and in no time had fashioned a card identifying her as Rachel Sloane. Now we were really getting into a squishy legal area and on foreign soil, to boot.

On the drive toward Dunstable, Freddie phoned. Scalabrino got the phone from Billy and put it on speaker. Freddie had met a reporter from the London Daily Mail named Sean Borton, who was in Luton to get dirt on the Featherstonaughs. After a couple of rounds at the pub, he told Freddie he had learned the family was in dire straits financially and was trying to sell off a number of properties to keep creditors and the taxman at bay. Freddie planned to ply him with more beer to get details.

Of course, that triggered a chorus of "Taxman" in my head. I was into the third verse when we pulled up at the psychiatric facility and Vi hopped out.

Scalabrino was going to wait around to see what Vi found out about Jasmine, but Lena called for pickup. She had gotten nowhere talking with Bitsy's husband, who had no idea about the whereabouts of any diary. His wife had never mentioned one.

Lena was happy to rejoin the group. The place had creeped her out a bit. She described it as a drafty old house that looked like it needed quite a few repairs. The husband seemed out of it, she reported; he kept calling for a servant he called Buffington who wasn't there.

The shit hit the fan when Scalabrino got a frantic call from one of his minions staking out the warehouse. We didn't hear the conversation, but the boss went white and muttered only, "Report back." Then he hung up.

"I have to get back to London," he said. "Mr. Biersovich will come with me. Vi will make arrangements for the rest of the group to stay the night in Luton. Billy, drop us at the airport, then report in later."

Scalabrino offered no explanation. Lena didn't like it, but she had little say in the matter. We were deposited at the Luton terminal. Scalabrino ordered Billy to contact Joe T and have him run the show locally, then Billy drove off with Lena. Scalabrino hired another driver who took us back to London.

We sat in the back seat silently until he asked to see my notepad and a pen. On a blank page, he wrote, "Explosion at warehouse."

I gave him a puzzled look, but he was silent and shook his head.

Our driver couldn't get within two blocks of the building. Knightsbridge was cordoned off, with police cars blocking the road. Two fire engines and an ambulance were also at the scene.

We got out and walked up to the barricade. "What happened?" I asked a gawker.

"Something blew up in a building over there. May have been a boiler," he said.

"Anyone hurt?"

He shrugged.

Scalabrino took off down the sidewalk and rang a number on his mobile. He grunted a few times then hailed a cab for us. It took us back to the apartment.

He was mixing a drink when he finally let me in on developments.

"There was an explosion in the building. My men were watching it via video feed. They saw someone creeping about the ground floor, then he disappeared. A few moments later, the explosion."

"A bomb?" I asked.

"Something like that. Getting reports that it seriously injured the intruder. Nearby shop owners thought a gas line had blown and were afraid of fire."

"Who was the intruder?"

"Trying to find that out now," Scalabrino said.

"Maybe the murderer," I opined.

"No doubt."

Well into our first round of drinks, Scalabrino got a call from Gregor, one of the men watching the building. He apparently had good connections at the hospital because he learned that the injured man was a habitual safecracker named Arnie Dobbs.

"That's the same last name as the lawyer!" I said. "Beaton Dobbs."

"I think we found our connection," Scalabrino said. "Now to find the lawyer."

JOE T SPENT the evening hunting Beany Dobbs after getting filled in by Scalabrino. The lawyer had disappeared, raising even more suspicion. Vi, posing as a relative, had learned that Jasmine Sloane was committed by Hugh Leicester. Lena said that's the name of Bitsy's husband, but she was doubtful that he had enough wherewithal to commit anyone. He himself should be committed, she added.

Scalabrino asked Vi to return the next day and get a description of Hugh Leicester from the facility. Lena was to return to the Leicester residence and quiz Hugh again, along with Bitsy if available.

An underling I didn't know arrived at the apartment and reported to Scalabrino. His name was Tomas. He said the warehouse building was now under round-the-clock watch following the explosion, and no one was being allowed near it. He was attempting to speak with the detective constable in charge of the case, someone named Huntington.

"That's my detective!" I cried.

"You've spoken with him?" Scalabrino asked.

"Yes. He was on the case when Stony was killed. Also the architect."

"We need to visit him tomorrow, Mr. Biersovich."

"I'm not sure he would tell us anything."

"Oh, you'd be surprised," Scalabrino said with a grin.

There were no more reports that evening. The crew in Luton was either too busy to phone in or had nothing to offer. We turned in early with the notion that the next day would be quite busy again.

SOMETIME IN the wee hours, I was awakened by voices. I glanced at the clock—2:45 a.m. Staggering down the hall half-asleep, I entered the game room to find Scalabrino in a heated conversation with someone on the phone. He had the speaker on and I heard Joe T advising the boss to pull up stakes.

"This is not an option, Joseph!" he said vehemently.

"Johnny, I know you had your heart set on that location, but there are just too many obstacles. People are getting bumped off right and left because of some secret in that building. I don't want our folks to be the next victims."

"There is little likelihood of that."

"I'm telling you I've been running into a brick wall up here. No one knows anything, or if they do know something, they're not telling. Miss Sloane is practically comatose, the guy who committed her—"

"Supposedly."

"—supposedly committed her is an imbecile barely capable of tying his own shoelaces. The shyster lawyer has scrammed. You talked to John Featherstonaugh—he doesn't know anything."

"What about the financial angle."

"What, you mean what the reporter found out? That may or may not have anything to do with the building. You know reporters—they're probably just inventing a scandal to sell papers."

"What if the explosion is tied into an insurance scam. I feel we're on the verge of a breakthrough, Joseph."

"The only thing breaking is my back from running around up here and banging into brick walls."

Scalabrino finally looked up and noticed me in the room. "We'll discuss this further in the morning. For now, stick to the agenda." Then he hung up without a goodbye.

"Dissension in the ranks?" I asked.

"Joseph feels the cost-benefit ratio is not in our favor."

I went back to bed in total agreement with Joe T. And the next day was destined to prove us right.

34

Wednesday, April 18

Scalabrino woke me up way too early after a fitful night's sleep. I had finally fallen into deep slumber and was on a snorkeling vacation with my brother when rudely awakened.

Apparently, he did the same with the rest of the troupe up in Luton, giving them their marching orders for the day. Our mission was to delve into the blast at the warehouse via a visit to Detective Constable Huntington.

Perhaps in America the boss had police contacts that would fill him in on open cases. But I didn't see that happening in Britain. Sometimes his arrogance, or should I say naiveté, astonished me.

Nevertheless, there we were at the West End Central Police Station by 9 a.m., waiting for an audience with Huntington on the premise that we knew something about the warehouse explosion.

Of course, I was ordered to withhold our trump card. No mention of the diary, Scalabrino commanded. However, I wasn't sure how to tie all the murders and mayhem together without it.

As expected, Huntington was tight-lipped about the ongoing investigation. We did offer some assistance by clueing him in to the identity of the bomber. Relative of the lawyer who's keeping one of the owners of the building sequestered, against her will, we suspected.

Interesting, Huntington nodded. He left the room for a few minutes.

"Why don't we just tell him about the diary?" I whispered.

"That's our ace in the hole," Scalabrino replied. "We need to save that for when we really need it."

I thought we should lay out all our cards, have the police do the legwork. After all, the main goal was to get the building purchased, however that would transpire. What difference did it make if the cops found the diary, cleared up the mystery and propelled the sale forward?

When Huntington returned, Scalabrino pushed him to investigate some of the more suspicious players in Luton: Beany Dobbs, perhaps the brother of the bomber; Marston, the probable ex-con; and Hugh Leicester, husband of Bitsy and supposed committer of Jasmine Sloane.

Of course, Huntington was disinclined to get involved in such an inquiry outside his jurisdiction, seeing as he had his hands full with London criminals running amuck. He referred us to Chief Inspector Haley McBaffin at the Bedfordshire Police Station and said he would call to let her know we were coming.

"How is Thomas Waters related to the owners?" Huntington asked.

"I don't know who that is or what his relationship is, if any."

Scalabrino asked who that was. I explained that he was the first victim found in the building, probably a homeless person who was in the wrong place at the wrong time.

While waiting outside the West End station for a ride, Scalabrino muttered, "Female inspector. Bah!" I had to agree with him on the concept, although I did remind him it was a woman who solved the robbery and nabbed the perps back at the home store.

He ordered me back up to Luton to get with the chief inspector. Why couldn't Joe T do it since he was already there, I asked. Because he's busy, was the reply.

So I was back on a shuttle heading up to the Bedfordshire Police Station north of Luton, wondering once again whether the job was worth the hassle. The pay was certainly good, more than I could get in the writing trade. And I was near my honey babe—speaking of which, I had forgotten to call the previous evening and made a note to do that at my earliest convenience. I was beginning to wonder whether I would ever see Emmie again.

Inspector McBaffin was not as I expected—a thick, rough woman who looked like she could wrangle steers. No, she was a vision right out of a Victoria's Secret catalogue, except in full police uniform.

Without Scalabrino there to put the reins on me, I debated whether to spill the beans about the diary and our suspicion that it was an essential clue to all the murders and assaults.

McBaffin had little time to chat, however, and appeared in a rush to get to more important matters. She seemed reluctant to solve Huntington's case for him, even though locals figured prominently in it.

Lacking action from her, I called Joe T to see what was afoot. He was still on a quest to find the lawyer, and the others had been dispatched to their assigned spots: Freddie gathering more dirt at the bar, Vi at the sanitarium, Lena at the Leicesters' and others elsewhere. The local crew now seemed to have grown to eleven people doing legwork. He told me to sit tight and he would have a job for me soon.

It was too early to call Emmie, so I picked up a copy of Luton Today and combed the want ads. Might as well shop while waiting for orders, I reasoned.

The rummage sale I selected was being conducted on the sidewalk of a flat near the town center. I suspected the owners were well into their 80s because the merchandise offered was beyond antique. I briefly considered a green Bakelite radio, but cracks in the case detracted from its worth. And, of course, it didn't work.

On the musical front, I managed to walk away with some sleeveless 45s: Little Richard, Chubby Checker, the Temptations and a few R&B artists I had never before considered. Seven discs cost me less than two pounds, a steal in any genre.

After a quick lunch at a nearby pub, I called Joe T because I was getting antsy. Hanging around Luton with nothing to do was tiring.

"I was just about to call you. Get down to the Luton jail and bail your buddy out," Joe T said.

"What? What the hell are you talking about?"

"Bar brawl. Go fetch him." Joe T hung up on me.

I suppose I shouldn't be surprised. It wasn't the first time I had to spring Freddie. Of course, the incident in Las Vegas "wasn't his fault," or so he claimed. I stewed all the way there in the taxi, vowing I would force him to grow up if it was the last thing I did.

Naturally, "It's not my fault" were the first words out of his mouth. Freddie looked the worse for wear, with a developing black eye, torn shirt and tissues stuffed up both nostrils. The jail medic had examined him and pronounced a broken nose. Served him right, I felt.

We repaired to a tea shop down the block, where Freddie laid out his sordid tale.

"So I was hanging with Sean Borton, the reporter. He was showing me how to play darts—he called them arrows—and I was teaching him the finer points of beer pong. He was still interviewing folks about the Featherstonaughs to find out whether they were owed any money. Quite a few, it turns out, did work on their estate. Including this one guy called Emerson...Enderman..."

"Enthoven?" I suggested.

"Yeah, that's it. Enthoven. Apparently, he was on retainer to work on the grounds and hadn't been paid in like six months. But when Borton asked why he continued to work for them when they hadn't paid, he got upset. I mean, he went ballistic. Then stuff started flying and I caught a fist or two."

"Why did he get mad? Exactly what did he ask him?"

"Something like: 'Are you hiding a reason for your work there for no pay?' Seemed innocuous enough."

"Enthoven was Stony's friend. In fact, Stony helped him out sometimes."

"Oh. So you think this relates to the brother?"

"Has to," I said. "And we know Stony was hiding a secret reason for not wanting to sell the warehouse. Where is Borton now?"

Freddie chuckled. "Think he went back to London. He wound up with an ankle sprain and probably has to get crutches to get around. Not to mention he was beat to hell by Enthoven. I just got in the way trying to break up the fight."

"Was Enthoven arrested?" I asked.

"Not surprisingly, they let him go."

I made some notes and decided we needed to look more into the landscaper's background before confronting him again. He was a hothead, perhaps capable of murder. But my researcher was off on another assignment.

"We need to go get Lena. She's at the Featherstonaugh sister's house. Know where that is?"

"Nope," Freddie answered. "But everyone in this town knows the family." He flagged down a waitress and quickly got the address. We took a cab up to the Leicester house and asked the driver to wait.

My second surprise of the day lay behind the front door.

35

S he's not here."

Mrs. Leicester was standing in the doorway of her two-story home on a lane a couple of miles from the main Featherstonaugh estate. Compared to the family manse, it was a modest home, a bit weather-beaten and obviously in need of Enthoven's expertise.

"Are you sure?" I asked. "Because she was supposed to be meeting with your husband this morning..."

"Hugh is off fishing for the day. Margate," Bitsy said.

"And Lena hasn't been here this morning?"

"No, haven't seen her," she replied, shaking her head.

I looked around, stalling for time, wondering where the hell Lena had gone off to instead of there. Had she met with Hugh and gone fishing with him? Possible but highly unlikely.

We thanked Bitsy and returned to the cab.

"Where to?" the driver asked.

I held up a finger while I dialed Joe T.

"She's not here," I reported. "Wife says she hasn't been around today. Husband is off fishing apparently."

"Fishing?" he replied. "Whereabouts?"

"Margate, I think she said."

"Something's fishy," he said. "No pun intended."

"Yeah, it's not like Lena to just wander off without a word."

"Not only that, I just came from the lawyer's house. Wife says *he's* out fishing too. Margate."

In the traditional mystery, here's the spot where it's reported that the plot thickened. Even Freddie could smell a rat.

"Somebody's lying," Freddie said.

"Or they're in cahoots," I added.

177

Joe T said he would send someone to Margate, on the North Sea east of London, to check it out. Meanwhile, Vi had found something I needed to see. Joe T told me to get over to the sanitarium pronto and leave Freddie to watch Hugh's house, in case he returned or Lena showed up. As an aside, he said he learned that Arnie Dobbs had died of his injuries a short while ago.

Vi met me at the door and ushered me into the visitors' waiting room. She gave me a copy of a letter she found in Jasmine's prayer book. She had no idea what it meant but thought it might be an important clue. Jasmine herself was still incommunicado with no prospect of providing any meaningful help in the near future.

The letter was bizarre, to say the least. It was handwritten by John Randolph Featherstonaugh to his wife, mother of Stony and the other siblings. It read:

My Love,
The Future is Uncertain but it is Assured.
Children will be Protected, as sure as a Carom pots a Red.
The Childhood Playground is a Haven for their Future.
A Future that's Impregnable.
A Future that's Secured in War and Peace.

JRF
6-1-70
12-8-30

At first reading it didn't make much sense, other than being an assurance that the children's future was secured by something the elder Featherstonaugh had done. But what? Two subsequent readings led me to the same conclusion.

It was cryptic and seemed to be all over the map—billiards, playground, a Tolstoy novel, a snippet of music? What did it all mean? Perhaps just an inside joke, I thought. Or more likely, the guy was insane.

The dates at the end of the letter were intriguing. One was well after the writer's death, the other 70 years in the past. There was a 40-year gap.

Or maybe it was a future date—2030. How would his children's future be assured when they would most certainly be dead themselves in 2030?

The concept of that far-future date triggered a song in my head—"In the Year 2525," a very old and prophetic tune about future doom. It seemed appropriate somehow.

"SHE'S ON THE MOVE." The call from Freddie came as I was puzzling over the meaning of the abstruse message. He relayed the car make and license number and suggested that someone needed to follow Bitsy around. I was talking with Joe T about doing just that when Bitsy strolled into the sanitarium and made a beeline for Jasmine's room. She didn't spot me. Joe T said he would drive over.

When Joe T arrived with the car, he told Vi to make sure nothing happened to Jasmine. Meanwhile, he and I would follow Bitsy Leicester. In a few minutes, she emerged from the facility and took off down the road. We followed.

It soon became apparent that she was driving down to London and she was in a hurry. I read the letter aloud to Joe T a couple of times, but he had no clue what it meant either.

Bitsy drove to an office building in Waterloo in the shadow of the London Eye, got out and went in. When Joe T called Scalabrino to update the scenario, the boss said he wanted us back at the apartment and he would send someone to cover.

The note didn't make any sense to Scalabrino either. He had heard rumblings that the old man was off his nut, but this cinched it for him. Scalabrino believed the diary still held the key, and possibly an actual key marked with G.

The scribbled musical notes intrigued me. But they didn't mean anything unless I heard them. I took the letter to the piano in the study and struck them as shown. The tune didn't ring a bell. A fact in the back of my mind was confirmed by a check of my notepad. The old man was an amateur musician, according to Charlene

McAllen, our real estate agent. So maybe this was a snippet of a song he knew or was writing.

I considered myself a fairly knowledgeable student of all things musical, but in this instance, I thought a bit of help wouldn't hurt. And I knew just the person to provide assistance.

36

Lawrence Hickey studied the notes and sounded them out several times, speeding up and slowing down the tempo. After a few minutes, he handed me back the paper.

"No, I'm afraid it's not from anything I know. It has similarities to several songs but not the exact sequence," Hick said. "It's just a phrase, perhaps pulled out of a longer work."

"That's what I thought," I replied. "He was sort of a musician so maybe it's a song he wrote."

"Ah, could be."

"Well, thanks anyway." As I turned to go, he stopped me and said he had one more present for me. It was a first pressing of the 45 version of "Badge" by Cream. He explained he had a gold master and several copies of the first pressing, so he thought I might like one for my collection. Boy, did I.

It was another reward for organizing his collection, which was now taking shape on newly acquired shelves in his living room. He had started with British Invasion, naturally, but already had quite a stunning assemblage.

It was getting on toward evening and still no word from Lena. Either she was onto something big or the murderer had struck again. Of course, I always tended to consider the worst possible conclusion the most likely. And I would have to deliver the eulogy in the dire vision I concocted.

Joe T had enlisted the assistance of the Bedfordshire police when there was still no sign of Lena in neither Luton nor Margate. No sign of the fishermen either.

Also unaccounted for was Marston, who had been followed and lost by one of Joe T's men. And the elusive Enthoven had holed up in his home and not ventured out, according to Freddie, who couldn't get him to talk.

Meanwhile, Bitsy Leicester had spent a couple hours at the office building in London before emerging and checking into the Covent Garden Hotel. Gregor was casing the joint.

Vi had given up trying to converse with Jasmine Sloane, who was being kept sedated by doctor's orders with no end in sight. Vi returned to the apartment in the evening to resume her party planning duties, then left for dinner with Scalabrino.

After a quick bite alone in the kitchen, I called Emmie to report that I still missed her enormously but there was no news on my imminent return. She expressed alarm when I told her Lena was MIA. She didn't want me to be the next to disappear.

There was little for me to do but wait for something to break. And attempt to decipher the peculiar ideogram penned by the Featherstonaugh forebear. I decided to break it down and examine each line for possible meanings.

My Love,

Obviously, this was addressed to his wife. Or was it? Did the old man have a bimbo on the side? Could it have been someone named Love? I didn't want to overanalyze this but given the context, it could be ambiguous.

The Future is Uncertain but it is Assured.

Well, that can be said for everyone. It's always uncertain. You don't know when you wake up whether it would be a normal day or...you would disappear somewhere. I speculated on Lena's whereabouts, worried that I would never get to hear that unique, raspy laugh again. A great sadness overcame me, then anger. I was determined to find her and banished thoughts of dire fates. She was OK, I told myself. Lena was just being Lena.

Anyway, "uncertain but assured." Could that mean insured? Maybe Featherstonaugh took out a large insurance policy to be shared with his survivors. But that probably would already be divided among the heirs. I made a note for Lena to check the life insurance records, if possible.

Children will be Protected, as sure as a Carom pots a Red.

Again, protected in a life insurance sense? Or protection in a bodyguard sense? And why the billiard reference? Does a pool hall or billiard table figure into the mix? Maybe there's cash hidden in one...

The Childhood Playground is a Haven for their Future.

What childhood playground? A park, perhaps, where something is buried? A chest full of pound notes, I wondered, or diamonds? A haven is a shelter of some sort. Could be a building situated on said playground. Conceivably a park building. Note: Check parks in London and Luton.

A Future that's Impregnable.

Impregnable...can't get pregnant? No, that's not what it means. Check the dictionary...ah, something that can withstand attack. So maybe a fort. Look for a park that has a fort in it...

A Future that's Secured in War and Peace.

Well, I wasn't about to read "War and Peace," so there had to be some other meaning behind this phrase. Perchance he meant through wartime and peacetime, something that held value regardless of the state of combat in Britain. Gold, of course. Gold bars, locked in a chest, buried in a fort in a park. A concept was starting to emerge.

And then I evaluated the notes.

This was the stumbling block. John Randolph Featherstonaugh had gone to the trouble of sketching this musical fragment for some reason but I could not fathom what that was. Unless this tune meant something to his children. Maybe it was something he played for them when they were kids, something that would put the rest of the clues into context.

At the piano, I played the notes again. And again. And still no spark of recognition. It wasn't rock, of that I was certain. A passage from an orchestral work, perhaps. Maybe one instrument's line, a bassoon floating behind the melody.

I needed a drink. The bar was open with no one to put the brakes on me. Besides, Scalabrino would approve. So I poured some bourbon over ice and sipped at the piano while staring at the notes.

They refused to speak to me. I decided to resume my line-by-line perusal and return to the music later.

JRF
6-1-70
12-8-30

JRF obviously was the writer's initials. Or was it? Could one of the children have written this letter? I looked through my notes and found another person with those initials: James Ronald Featherstonaugh, the second son. Was there any way this could have been written by the son and not the father? Didn't seem likely, but I had to consider every possibility.

Then the dates: June 1, 1970 and December 8, 1930 or perhaps 2030. That didn't seem right. The British wrote their dates differently, so it was probably 6th of January, 1970 and 12th of August, 1930 or 2030. If it was 1930, there was a 40-year gap between the dates. Why? It was 60 years if it was 2030.

Thinking about that far future date, I determined that the children probably would be dead by then, seeing as they were all pushing 70 except for Stony. Who was dead already. So it had to be 1930. What happened on August 12, 1930?

Again, another case where Lena's research expertise would come in handy.

When my glass ran dry, my conscience told me it would be bad form to refill it. I told my conscience to go screw itself—these were desperate times.

After rereading the letter several more times, I had amassed quite a few sheets of notes and questions. I counted 32 questions in all, none of them currently answered. Well, I consoled myself, at least I know what I don't know.

37

Thursday, April 19

My overnight sojourn was an adventure in music, naturally. I was part of an orchestra, playing cymbals. There were no notes on my pages, just bar after bar of rests. Finally, on the last page, there was a note for me to strike, but I was so unnerved that I missed my cue. The rest of the orchestra stopped and stared at me for botching my one note.

Scalabrino was drinking coffee and conversing on the phone when I entered the kitchen. Vi was making a proper English breakfast with eggs, toast, sausage, mushrooms, stewed tomatoes and baked beans. It looked like she was expecting a crowd.

"Good morning, Mr. Biersovich," Scalabrino said after ending his conversation. "I trust you slept well."

"Somewhat."

"We have another busy day ahead of us. Joseph suddenly has a dearth of candidates to interview, and our Mrs. Leicester has not emerged as yet. Any luck with that letter?"

"No, sir. Well, I have lots of questions but no answers. It looks like it may be a treasure map of sorts."

He considered this for a moment, then asked Vi if everything was ready. She said yes.

"Enjoy your breakfast, Mr. Biersovich," he said. "I will contact you in a while. Have your phone handy." And he got up, kissed Vi square on the lips and left. Vi smiled at me, told me to have as much as I wanted and followed him out of the kitchen.

I knew wondering about their relationship wasn't conducive to finding Lena or solving the diary mystery, but I couldn't help it. Was Vi his girlfriend? Or just one of many he stashed around the globe? She seemed to work for him, so she must have screwed her way to the top...

My ringing phone interrupted my reverie. Freddie sounded breathless, like he had been running. He couldn't talk but said something big was happening and he'd call back as soon as he could. He didn't say whether Joe T was in on it, so I phoned him to find out what was going on. Joe T hadn't heard a thing and also wondered what it was. I told him I'd call when Freddie clued me in on the details.

While thoroughly stuffing myself with the bounty of breakfast goodies, I briefly considered trying to conduct my own computer research on the machine in the office. I almost laughed out loud at myself. No, that wouldn't work. Best to keep hammering away at it with a stream-of-consciousness approach and hope for divine inspiration.

There were only two ways to get me out of this mess. One, convince Scalabrino that I couldn't solve it. Two, solve it.

In previous cases, I had been inspired by music in some way, so I thought it might work here. When in Britain...

I began running through every song I could remember from the British Invasion era—Beatles, Stones, BeeGees, Hollies, Kinks, Who, Herman's Hermits, Dave Clark Five, Yardbirds, Donovan, Gerry and the Pacemakers. None of the tunes triggered a connection. I was trying to force the type of inspiration that had led me to solutions in previous cases, but I knew it didn't work that way. It seemed I had to wait for the brainstorm to hit me when I least expected it.

Then I thought why not confront the siblings directly and ask them where they thought this treasure was buried. Of course, one of them might be the killer, in which case possession of this letter could prove fatal.

There was still the matter of the diary. Did it contain some key to the meaning of the letter? Or perhaps different information than the letter? Maybe the mother got the letter, figured out what it meant, re-buried the treasure elsewhere and left the new key, one marked with G, in her diary.

What did the G stand for? None of the principals' names started with that letter. Could be the initial for a bank, where a lock box held the treasure, or the location of such. Then again, since I had deduced that the booty might be hidden in a park, it could be the key to a park building.

I was going to have to start hitting the bottle again if I kept coming up with all these questions. There was no one to bounce ideas off of, as I had in previous cases. If Lena didn't get back soon…

Then what?

Then I'd just have to worry all the longer, naturally. Could be that Freddie had found out where Lena was and was on his way to meet her. I preferred to think that than the other possibilities.

For a short moment, I considered calling Tina, but seeing as it was in the wee hours back in the U.S., that wouldn't be a good idea. Tina had a pretty sharp tongue when awakened too early. I found that out one time when I inadvertently dialed her number instead of Lena's when I was up pre-dawn for my first estate sale.

I had scribbled another dozen questions by the time Scalabrino called and ordered me down to the police station. Our old friend Bitsy was there with a lawyer, trying to get access to the warehouse.

After waiting around for 20 minutes, I saw her walking out of Huntington's office with her lawyer and the detective constable in procession.

"Good morning, Mrs. Leicester," I said. "Can I have a word?"

"Not now," she replied brusquely. "Off to assess the damage."

"Mind if I tag along?"

She looked me up and down, then said, "That would be all right. After all, you need to ascertain that the building is still purchase worthy." We piled into a police van that Huntington called to the front of the station and were escorted by another patrol car to the warehouse.

Arriving at the front door, I looked around to see where Scalabrino's men were posted. I knew they were watching but couldn't spot them right off the bat.

There was nothing apparently amiss on the ground floor. The entourage went up the back stairs to the third floor, where the scene of carnage lay undisturbed. A chalk outline with an overlapping stain of blood the circumference of a basketball was situated near a somewhat crumpled wall in one of the offices. Across from it was a blast zone with a gaping hole in the wall, splintered studs and a debris field. Arnie Dobbs apparently had been blown back against the far wall and suffered his fatal injuries as a result.

Aside from the walls, there seemed to be little structural damage. Bitsy gazed at the hole for an eternity before moving on and examining the walls in the other offices.

To all appearances satisfied that the building wasn't in danger of imminent collapse, Bitsy nodded and headed for the stairwell. Outside the door, I asked her whether there was some way to proceed with the sale.

"This is my solicitor, Mr. Canby," she said, indicating the heretofore silent man following in her wake. "We are meeting with my siblings and looking for a way forward. We shall be in touch." Then she and the lawyer piled into a taxi and left. Huntington asked whether I wanted a ride back to the station and I declined.

Joe T was interested to hear the details but had nothing to report on his end. No sign of Lena and no word from Freddie. He had spoken with Billy, who dropped Lena off the day before at the Leicesters' home. The cabbie said she got out at the curb and he was off before she approached the front door, if she did.

Standing on the sidewalk in front of the warehouse building, I once again gazed around me to try to spot the lookouts. A beam of light reflected into my eyes directed me across the road, and I followed the source. Sitting in a dark sedan were two men I didn't recognize. The driver rolled down the window and introduced himself as Xavier, his partner as Yancy.

"What's all that then?" Xavier asked, flicking his hand across the street.

"Mrs. Leicester, one of the owners, wanted to survey the damage. Big hole in an upstairs wall. That's about it."

"Is the building open now?" he asked.

"No, I don't think so. Police still have it locked down. Mrs. Leicester plans to get a repair crew in as soon as they give the go-ahead."

"Mmmm," he replied.

"Does Mr. Scalabrino have you stationed here round-the-clock?"

"Something like that," the one called Yancy mumbled.

"Good luck, then," I said and headed up the sidewalk to the Tube. I was sure there was no need to call Scalabrino because his minions X and Y would relate my conversation with them.

I was having a cup of tea at a shop down the street when Scalabrino called and threw yet another monkey wrench into the equation.

38

"Pack your bags, Mr. Biersovich," he said. "You're going home."

Although this was the news I had been waiting for practically since I arrived on British soil, I wasn't expecting it at this juncture, what with everything in flux. Especially Lena.

"Sir, why now? Nothing is settled yet, and I'm reluctant to leave until I find out where Lena is and if she's OK."

"I'm afraid there's nothing you can do right now except wait for the authorities to do their job. They are combing the countryside, but the trail is cold so far. I'm sending your friend Mr. Skelton back with you. Vi will phone you shortly with details." He hung up on me.

This short conversation filled me with dread. *Wait for the authorities to do their job.* That meant Joe T and gang had been unsuccessful, and Lena was truly gone. It could only mean she had become another victim of the murderer.

I made it to a men's room just in time to throw up all the tea and whatever stomach contents were left from breakfast. A sickening chill enveloped me, along with the realization that I probably had lost one of my closest friends. Because that's what Lena had become over the course of my brief employment at La Scala—a friend, plus the person I relied on most for help, particularly for research and computer work.

As I hung over the bowl and continued to empty my gut, I was convinced I finally and irrevocably had to quit the job, the one that had brought me close to the love of my life, Emmie. She would understand, I was certain. The job wasn't worth risking life and limb over, despite the nice paycheck and advancement in the store hierarchy.

Just as I was cleaning up and feeling some semblance of normal, Vi called with my itinerary. I had three hours to get packed and off to Heathrow, where Freddie would meet me for our flight back. I asked if there were any word on Lena. She said the Bedfordshire police had made it a priority.

The apartment seemed cold and foreboding when I returned. After packing my suitcase, I went to the north wing to look at Lena's quarters. It was a bit messy, with clothes on the chair, an unmade bed and a row of shopping bags lined up on the floor. I thought about straightening it up but couldn't even fathom stepping foot in her room. The pain in my gut returned.

At the appointed hour, I caught a shuttle to the airport, collected my ticket and made my way to my gate, a direct flight back to Minneapolis-St. Paul International Airport. About 20 minutes later, Freddie showed up with an uncharacteristic sober look. We sat in silence, waiting for the boarding announcement. The strains of British rock groups mingled with the general cacophony of rolling luggage and various languages spoken by fellow passengers.

Malaise had gripped me, despite the knowledge that I would soon be seeing Emmie's sweet face. It was still too early back home to call her and let her know I was on the way, however. And I still had so many unanswered questions.

"Freddie, what was that you were onto earlier when I called? Sounded like you were in a hurry to get somewhere."

"Oh, Enthoven finally emerged from his bungalow and said he was going to avenge his friend's death. Looked to me like he was going out on a landscaping job, though, so I didn't follow him."

Another piece of the puzzle that didn't quite fit. How was Enthoven going to avenge Stony's murder? And had he figured out who the killer was? I phoned Joe T and told him it might pay dividends to tail the landscaper.

As the boarding time approached, I headed to the men's room for the final pee. A song entered my head and I realized it was playing over the intercom in the bathroom. "Abacab," an old Genesis tune. Hadn't heard that one in years.

Then as I was washing up, some synapse snapped and triggered a memory, a twinkling of a concept that was dredged up from the far recesses of my gray matter. I pulled out my notepad and unfolded the copy of John Randolph Featherstonaugh's letter.

This time, the pieces fell into place. It made sense. I had it, the key to the treasure map. It was hiding in plain sight. Now what to do with it...

Racing out of the men's room, I barked at Freddie to grab his suitcase and follow me.

"Beers, I'm done," he responded. "I can't do any more here. I'm heading back."

"You're just going to leave Lena out in the cold," I said accusingly.

"Dude, the cops are looking for her. I wouldn't know where to begin."

"I'll tell you where to begin on the way back to London. Your decision, Freddie. But I'm going back." I rolled my suitcase down the concourse as quickly as I could without running over other fliers.

When I arrived at the taxi stand, Freddie came up behind me, panting.

"Dude, you running a hundred-meter dash or what?" He was bent over, trying to catch his breath, when our cab arrived.

On the ride back to the apartment, I outlined Freddie's extended duties, which would take him back to Luton. He was reluctant, but he had seen that look of determination on my face before, the one that told him I was on the verge of breaking a case wide open. Either that or my ideas would get laughed off the island. But for Lena it was worth the risk.

Scalabrino was shocked at first to learn that I had bolted the airport, but when I related my suspicions, he gave me his blessing. He was on his way to Luton, following Bitsy's car, and would assist with the continued interrogations.

Joe T was likewise surprised that I wasn't already over the ocean. When I suggested another area of research, he agreed to give it a go.

Meanwhile, I had a line of inquiry that would require an expert, and I knew just the guy.

GARRY NAUGHTON hadn't expected to hear from me again, what with the building shut down due to murders. I told him my suspicions and repeated Lena's conversation on what the architect found. He said it sounded plausible.

Next I trekked down to the West End police station to await an audience with Detective Constable Huntington. I would need his blessings to get back in the building and check out my theory.

It took a while, but I managed to convince him that I was onto something that merited investigation. The supporting documentation, some mine, some Lena's, sold him. An hour later, the three of us were standing in the warehouse, gazing at a blank wall. Naughton had made some measurements, consulted blueprints and nodded.

"Which of the siblings do you trust?" Huntington asked me.

"At the moment, none of them," I replied.

"Then we should proceed forthwith." Naughton concurred.

While the detective constable was summoning a team, I checked in with Joe T. Scalabrino had arrived and staked out Bitsy's house. Joe T's men had combed the grounds of Baron Featherstonaugh's estate and were now examining James Featherstonaugh's property, much to his chagrin. Then Joe T was heading to Bitsy's place.

In time, the crew arrived and set to work. Naughton directed, based on his best conjecture of where to begin. The din was deafening, and I barely heard my phone ringing.

Once again, Freddie was out of breath.

"I got it, Beers," he reported. "The cook said there was a dinner the night before and there was one couple attending."

"Bitsy and Hugh," I said.

"Bingo."

39

It was evening before the crew had broken through the wall and opened the safe. Yes, there was a safe, probably left over from when the building housed a bank, standing about four feet tall and three wide.

On a hunch, I provided what I thought was the combination and it opened on the first try.

Stacked inside it were hundreds of war bonds, some issued in London but most from Berlin. The old man had bet the children's future on Nazi war bonds, which probably were worth a few pounds strictly for the novelty factor. The British notes still had value but didn't add up to a fortune.

The picture became clear in my mind. Stony figured out where the treasure was buried but got waylaid before he could retrieve it. The perpetrator had killed two people to protect the "fortune" for himself. Or herself. That part was still a bit unclear, but I had narrowed down the suspects.

A bit later, with news from Luton, the cat was out of the bag.

Bitsy Leicester had refused to let Joe T into her house. He left, saying he was going to get a court order. Scalabrino continued to stake out her place and saw her leaving with a suitcase shortly thereafter. He and Billy followed her; Joe T returned to conduct his search unobstructed.

It didn't take him long to find the locked door leading to the cellar, where Lena and Hugh had been imprisoned. They were tired but otherwise in good health, Joe T reported. Lena said she could use a change of clothes and something to eat other than cheese and crackers.

Police joined the pursuit of Bitsy after they received the report of her captives. She was apprehended at a roadblock south of

Manchester. She apparently was fleeing to Scotland, where her accomplice had holed up.

Beany Dobbs was taken a short time later at his hotel room. He hadn't bothered to cover his tracks very well. His personalized license plate was a dead giveaway. So to speak. And in his trunk were the incriminating goods: a well-worn diary and a recently used, somewhat rusty cleaver.

Then the sordid plot began to unfold as each player tried to rat out the other in order to gain clemency. Dobbs was at a decided disadvantage, however, as he was the possessor of the fatal implement. He was quickly charged with two counts of first-degree murder and criminal conspiracy. Bitsy Leicester was charged as an accessory to murder, along with conspiracy and illegal imprisonment.

A codicil of the trust would eliminate Helen Marie Featherstonaugh Leicester from further profits or decision-making responsibilities "for acts of perjury, conspiracy to commit criminal activity or malfeasance." The brothers were appalled and disbelieving that she could participate in such a scheme.

Meanwhile, Jasmine Sloane was released from her commitment after it was determined that Hugh Leicester never set foot in the sanitarium. The committer was Beaton Dobbs, pretending to be Hugh. Nurses verified his identity from his booking mug. A count of false imprisonment was added to the mounting tally he faced.

Jasmine was able to confirm to police the gist of my story—that Stony had learned of the existence of the "treasure cache" from his mother's diary; that he must have let slip to Beaton Dobbs his knowledge of something hidden in the warehouse; that Stony had been murdered shortly thereafter, and Beany took over Jasmine's "care" on the pretense that he was Stony's solicitor.

Piecing together verbal clues from their separate statements, police learned that Beaton Dobbs enlisted Bitsy Leicester in a plan to extract the treasure, wherever it was hidden, and that this plot was hatched in a bedroom, where they were engaged in extramarital activities.

Meanwhile, David Enthoven, landscaper and friend of Samuel Keith "Stony" Perkins, had contacted Inland Revenue to report that the Featherstonaughs were claiming tax credits for leased farmland that was no longer being cultivated. He knew this from his survey of the grounds of the estate following a tip from Stony.

This was the scoop that the London reporter failed to extract from Enthoven.

My call to Emmie that evening was a relief to both of us. Yes, I was finally coming home. Vi had made the arrangements. Freddie, Lena and I would be together on an afternoon flight Saturday. I assured Emmie that there was no way I would miss this one.

LATE IN THE EVENING, Scalabrino assembled the team for a dinner at one of the tonier dining establishments in London. Lena had washed her ordeal away with a two-hour bubble bath and felt human again. She reported that Hugh wasn't the doddering fool she first thought. He was actually a riveting storyteller when you spent some time with him and had some fascinating tales of wartime heroics.

This was where the boss dropped the final bomb on our English adventure. He was discarding his plan to build a store in London. The whole episode had convinced him that operating outside the U.S. of A. would be problematic. Plus dealing with that family and its legal problems would keep the property tied up in the courts for years.

You bastard, I thought. You put us through all this, then drop it? That's it. That's the final straw.

I was mentally polishing off my resignation letter throughout the meal.

40

We had one more day to kill in London so we decided to do some tourist things. Lena had her fill of department stores and anything having to do with potential department stores. She suggested we take a train ride in the country to a palace she heard about where we could have cocktails and a relaxing lunch.

Freddie and I argued the whole trip. He harangued me to return to the newspaper, as he had done on countless previous occasions. I assured him that wherever I went, it wouldn't entail printing words on dead trees.

Arriving at Hampton Court Palace, Lena led the way, following a crowd of visitors. Freddie continued his verbal assault, unwilling to drop his quest for my return to the Herald.

"You don't have a real plan, do you?" he asked.

"There's a plan."

"So what are you going to do when you resign from the store? Tell me. I'm keen to know."

There was no plan, actually, so I remained silent. All I knew was I had to escape, somehow, some way.

"I gotta go check on sumpin'," Lena said. "Just go through that hedge ovah yondah an' I'll meet ya at da cafe."

We headed through a gap in a high hedge, following an elderly couple who looked like they were hungry and thirsty.

"Beers, what's your middle name? What's the A stand for?" Freddie asked.

"Alfred."

"Alfred? No shit? I think I'm going to start calling you...Freddie!"

"No, you're not."

"Sure I am, Freddie."

"Then I guess I won't be speaking to you anymore."

"Come on, Beers. You used to have a sense of humor."

"And I used to have a friend named Freddie who wasn't a total wack job. Oh wait..."

"Har-de-har. Your life would be so dull without me."

"Dull is looking more appealing all the time. Besides which, since I'm a figment of your sleeping imagination..."

"I've sorta dropped that theory," Freddie said.

"Oh, really? What a shame. It was such a reasonable notion," I said in my most sarcastic tone.

"You just have no sense of humor. I've come to the conclusion that I'm funny. You just don't appreciate it."

"Funny looking, maybe."

At that point I looked up and realized we had been traveling through the hedge for some ways, turning a couple of times. There was no exit in sight, just more hedges curving away in the distance.

"Freddie, I think we're lost."

He looked behind us. "I'll ask that girl...Excuse me, miss, is this the way to the cafe?"

The woman laughed. "I'm sure it's in here somewhere." She giggled some more, then headed off ahead of us.

"That was strange," Freddie said.

We followed the woman for a ways until she went left at a junction. We considered left or right, then went right. The path twisted some more and we hit another junction.

"Freddie, I think we're in a maze."

"No shit, Sherlock. What gave it away?"

After wandering around a bit more, I stopped another elderly couple and asked whether they knew which way to go. They said they were as lost as we were.

"I've got an idea," Freddie said. "If we keep going right, we should eventually reach an exit."

"And if we hit a dead end?"

"Just backtrack and go right again."

We tried that and still didn't find a way out. Finally, we heard a familiar voice behind us.

"You guys wanna go eat or ya gonna fool around in heah all day?" Lena had a wicked grin on her face.

"Ha ha, very funny," I said. "Can we get out of here now?" She led the way, referring to a map she had acquired, and we found the path to freedom.

"Nice prank," Freddie said.

"Yeah," Lena replied, "Well, I owed ya one." So she had gotten her revenge for the trick cigar, plus pulling a fast one on Freddie as a bonus. Two for one. Fair enough.

Fifteen minutes later we were seated at a cafe enjoying a cold draft and celebrating the end of our London assignment.

"So we never did hear how you figured this one out," Freddie said.

"Yeah," Lena added. "I missed some stuff while I was playin' tic-tac-toe wit' Hugh."

"All right. I'll fill in the gaps," I said. "But Freddie, you'll have to buy another round because this may take a while."

"Good," Lena said. "Den I got sumpin' you may find interestin'." Her Cheshire grin returned.

41

We were looking for a diary but never found it. Jasmine said Stony read something in his mother's diary that indicated the warehouse building held the key to his future. We had no clue about what that was because Jasmine couldn't tell us where the diary was."

"She was drugged," Freddie said.

"Essentially, yeah. Someone was keeping her doped up to prevent her from spilling the beans about the hidden treasure. Because that's what it was, basically."

"Not much of a treasure, if ya ax me," Lena opined.

"Well, nobody knew that until we opened that safe. The old man thought he was investing in their future with war bonds. He apparently thought the Nazis had a better chance of winning than the Allies, since he seemed to invest heavily in German bonds."

"What a blunder," Freddie said.

"And two people got murdered over a piddling amount of money," I added. "Actually, three. Not to mention the mugging of our first property agent, which I think was also connected."

"Wait, what do you mean three? Who else got killed?" Freddie asked.

"I'll explain in a bit."

"How is Charlene doin'?" Lena asked.

"Last I heard she was fine. I guess we should call her before we leave town and give her the bad news. All that work, and injuries, and no commission."

"So how did you figure out where that safe was?" Freddie asked.

"It was the note in Jasmine's prayer book," I said. "It must be what Stony's mother based her diary entry on, the letter from her husband. It was very cryptic, full of stuff that only someone like Stony could figure out. Or I guess me also."

"How so?"

"Old man Featherstonaugh was apparently quite a character. He fancied himself a shrewd businessman and was somewhat of a musician as well. His son John told me he would entertain clients in pubs with rounds of beer, followed by sing-alongs once they got loopy enough. He played piano and was fairly accomplished at it.

"Unfortunately, none of his children had a musical inclination, so if they saw the letter, it didn't mean much to them. However, after he passed on, Stony, the child of his widow and her second husband, was himself a musician."

"What happened to the wife's second husband?" Freddie asked.

"Lived only about a year after they married. Long enough to get her pregnant with Stony. The Featherstonaughs apparently didn't consider Stony a real sibling, but the mother was able to amend the trust and add him in, along with Jasmine much later. I guess that created some animosity."

"So what's da musical connection?" Lena asked.

"The notes J.R. Featherstonaugh scribbled in his letter," I said. "At first I thought it could be a snippet from some song, which would provide a clue to the location of the goods. But I showed it to Hick—the retired deejay—and he couldn't place it. We concluded it was possibly something Featherstonaugh was writing himself.

"When I met with Hick, he gave me another item from his disc collection, a gold master of an old Cream tune called 'Badge.' Then I heard a song in the airport that clicked the final tumbler into place."

"What song?" Freddie asked.

"It was 'Abacab,' an old Genesis number. That triggered a vague memory about songs that can be written as notes. 'Badge' and 'Abacab' are two such songs—you can write out the letters in the song names as notes on the staff.

"See, here's the staff." I pulled the letter from my notepad. "If you had a band class you'll see Every Good Boy Deserves Favor. That's the notes of the lines of the staff: E, G, B, D, F. The spaces are F, A, C and E.

"So if you look at the musical passage as letters instead of notes, you get a phrase."

"What phrase?" Lena asked.

"F-A-C-E E B-A-C-rest-E-D-G-E."

"Rest?"

"Yeah, there was a rest in place of the letter that couldn't be represented on the musical staff. So the message was face east, back edge."

"What does that mean?"

"Taken in context with the rest of the note, he was talking about the back side of the warehouse, facing east. The passage was also in the key of G major—one sharp. That was the missing G key that Jasmine said Stony mentioned. Charlene McAllen said J.R. Featherstonaugh called the warehouse space a sharp, instead of a flat. Odd sense of humor. And Lena, you remember the architect said something didn't jibe with the measurements of the building when he was looking at the first floor?"

"Yeah. Some missing space or sumpin'."

"Exactly. The missing space was due to the wall being moved forward several feet to accommodate a safe. It was walled up at the back of the building. The safe was a leftover from when the place was used as a bank. The old man kept the safe, put his bonds in it, then walled it up for safekeeping, no pun intended."

"That's nuts."

"He obviously concocted this scheme during World War II. He thought the Nazis were going to overwhelm Britain and all of Europe. He saw the war bonds as a good investment. He died in 1944, before his future endowment turned to vapor."

"His thinking must have been that Britain had just instituted a purchase tax on luxury goods. Featherstonaugh thought the handwriting was on the wall—the rich would become the middle class pretty soon with all the taxes levied on them. He was afraid investments would be the next revenue target, so he hid the bonds, hoping they would increase in value down the line and his children would figure out a way to avoid the taxes. Must run in the family because the children are trying to elude the taxman themselves in other ways."

"How you find all dis out?" Lena asked.

"You won't believe it if I told you, but I'm not going to tell you. Anyway, Featherstonaugh had some strange phrases in his letter that took me a long time to figure out." I pointed to the letter. "Take this for example: 'As sure as a carom pots a red.' You know what snooker is? That's an allusion to billiards, but it's got nothing to do with snooker tables."

"How so?"

"A carom is when a ball is bounced off a cushion. Pool players sometimes call that a bank shot. Bank. So it was a hidden reference to a bank. The safe is a leftover from a bank housed in that building. He also refers to a childhood playground. The young Featherstonaughs used to play in the offices on the third floor.

"The letter said the future was 'impregnable,' like a safe. And it says the future is secured in war and peace. I thought at first he might have been referring to the novel."

"Nevah read dat."

"It's a long one. No, he was referring to the bonds, war bonds that would be valuable, or so he thought, when peacetime arrived. He held out hope that the German government would eventually make good on the war bonds, even though they were issued by the Nazis."

"Miscalculation," Freddie said.

"No lie. He died and the widow soon remarried. Stony was born in 1950. But no one knew about the war bonds. The exact nature of the 'treasure' remained unknown to both Stony and his mother. Until Stony figured it out, obviously.

"The final pieces of the puzzle were the number sequences at the end of the letter. I thought they were dates. Well, the first one is a date, Jan. 6, 1970. That was apparently the date the old man designated as redemption date for the bonds. The other numbers, 12-8-30, didn't make much sense as a date, either 1930, which was well before World War II, or 2030, when all the children would be long dead. So I figured it had to be the combination to the safe."

"Wow. And you got all that from hearing a song in the airport."

"The mind works in mysterious ways," I said. "Then there was the matter of the murder weapon for both Stony and Greene, the architect. Remember I had you check who attended a dinner the night before the first murder?"

"Yeah, Mr. and Mrs. Leicester."

"When Scalabrino and I visited a few days later, I recalled the cook arrived with a boxful of groceries, including a brand new cleaver. Someone had lifted the old one. I think it was Bitsy, who passed it on to her accomplice, Beany."

"Beany, Bitsy, Stony...sounds like a gang a cartoon charactahs."

"Blimey! What a couple of scrotes!" Freddie said.

"Wayah ya get dat talk?" Lena asked.

"Picked up a few idioms while I was hanging with the Mirror guy."

"Ya might wanna put 'em back down like right quick," she responded.

"You said three murders," Freddie said. "Who else got stiffed?"

"Oh, right. The first murder, actually. We thought he was a vagrant who happened to be in the building and was killed. Turns out he was a sometimes bandmate of Stony. Name of Thomas Waters. They called him Tom-Tom because he played drums. He owned the keyboard Stony used when they played occasional gigs. Police are working to pin his murder on Beany and Bitsy also."

"Sheesh."

"Stony probably enlisted his aid in searching for the treasure. Which the siblings obviously objected to."

"No kidding."

"So I guess we're leavin' town befoah da big pawty tamorrah night."

"I kept waiting for Vi to invite us but since we leave at 2...I'm ready to go home anyway," I said.

"Well, Scalabrino an' his wife need some time ta themselves, I guess," Lena replied.

"Wife?" Freddie and I said in unison.

"What wife?" I asked.

"Vi, of course."

Epilogue

I suppose I should have put the clues together earlier, but I was preoccupied with that other thing. The full-on smooch should have been a giveaway. Scalabrino had never mentioned anything about a wife and in my several visits to his mansion, Vi wasn't around. Perhaps it was strictly a long-distance relationship.

My own long-distance relationship finally came to a conclusion. Emmie and I enjoyed an all-day date on Sunday: a picnic, a visit to a cheese farm in Wisconsin, then a movie, some wine and a lot of time alone together.

I had managed to make a few friends during my fortnight in London. While Lena and Freddie were taking a ride on the newly opened London Eye, an attraction too tall for my tastes, I paid one last visit to the Mercy Beats record shop, where Lawrence Hickey was visiting his niece, Jillian. I thanked them for their assistance in solving the case because without that disc Hick gave me, I might never have put the pieces together. We promised to stay in touch.

At Edgingham's, Cerise was glad to see me but sorry to learn I was leaving. She also promised to stay in touch, especially since she and her boyfriend were planning to visit the States in the fall. I warned her that early fall would be more colorful and weather-friendly if the Twin Cities were on her itinerary.

Enthoven dropped all charges against Freddie due to the bar brawl, seeing as Freddie had been a small help in nabbing his friend Stony's killer.

My newly cleaned shirt and jacket finally arrived an hour before we left for the airport with a note from Jasmine: Sorry so late. Cleaners were closed—off fishing in Margate.

Freddie's reporter friend filled in the rest of the story when news of the murder arrests broke. His exposé on the Featherstonaughs' mythical farm leasing operation garnered an inside spread, with one David Enthoven supplying much of the corroborating material.

John Featherstonaugh, as primary landowner, had concocted the scheme, with participation from his CPA and brother, James, who cooked the books and filed phony lease papers for several years. Sister Helen Leicester was also part of the plot; she arranged for tilling and posting of acreage to maintain the pretense of occupancy.

Not in on the plot: Samuel "Stony" Perkins, who had no share in the proceeds and apparently no knowledge of the program. Enthoven, believing his friend and sometimes assistant Stony was part of the deal, kept quiet about it until the murder, when he figured out whodunit.

Before leaving Britain, Lena had lined up an appointment to get her tattoo removed upon her return to the Twin Cities. She warned me not to mention it to anyone, if I knew what was good for me.

THE IDENTITY of the mysterious Raleigh she had been surreptitiously communicating with became apparent when we landed. It was her brother, who arrived at the airport to pick her up and would be in town for a week. The secret lover I envisioned turned out to be a dentist from Baton Rouge. He was quite an entertaining storyteller, based on a meal and drinks Emmie and I shared with them one evening at Lena's condo.

Back at La Scala, Salmon Foster wasn't happy about it, but I took another week off to get my head straight and figure out what I wanted to do. Leaving the store was a foregone conclusion. I had enough savings socked away to tide me over until I landed another remunerative gig.

Still, I had that age-old dilemma: what next?

Tina encouraged me to try something else, like she had. It might give me a better appreciation of how good I had it at La Scala, she said.

Freddie continued his campaign to get me back into reporting, which I resisted steadfastly. If there was one thing I wanted to do even less than store security, it would be returning to newspaper work.

Unfortunately, when I looked at my skill set, it was lacking in one vital area—computer savvy. Everyone wanted employees who could do email, word processing, spreadsheets and other electronic functions. I even thought about going back to school to take some computer courses, get up to speed with the requirements of the modern workforce, but that was another thing I was reluctant to do.

Emmie playfully suggested I get Scalabrino to adopt me, then I wouldn't have to worry about money and maybe he'd think twice about putting me in risky situations.

I did register with the state job commission but based on my experience, I could choose from data entry clerk, mailroom clerk or filing clerk. Ugh.

So until that ideal position comes along—something like executive rock 'n' roll archivist to the stars—I'm keeping my day job. The pay is good, I'm close to the girl of my dreams and only occasionally am I at risk of losing life and limb.

But in my file cabinet, there's a cassette ready to be popped into the player for that magical day when I can leave it all behind, crank up the music and walk out of the office singing: *Take this job and shove it...*

♫

The adventures of Jim "Beers" Biersovich are made possible by folks who both inspire me and make me work harder.

I have to mention a great friend and lifelong inspiration, Rosa Mansur Dunn, who passed away all too soon. Before there was Beers, she was encouraging me to write by her enthusiasm and support. I included one of her many *bon mots* in the story.

Of course, there is my editor, the incomparable Dana Davis, whose skills with the blue pen are unmatched in the known universe, and perhaps elsewhere. Her keen eye for detail and nuance challenge me to hone the prose to perfection. She tries, but I know I always fall short.

Then there is my wife, Jeanne Anne, who is a lot funnier than I could ever be. I would put her in the series as a character but I probably wouldn't survive to continue writing.

As always, I hope you have been entertained by my journey into mystery and music.

Discover the roots of the Jim Biersovich story. *First Case of Beers*, the initial title in the series, introduces Beers, Lena, Tina, Freddie and the rest of the wacky crew trying to keep the ship of commerce La Scala afloat.

It's Christmas season at the turn of the Millennium. A vandal is causing mayhem in the department store where Beers is head of security.

Although he's not really qualified—his training was as a sportswriter—Beers is charged with finding out who is assaulting Johnny Scalabrino's business. A cryptic clue left at the scene of each incident baffles the amateur sleuth. In the end, his knowledge of classic rock music reveals the key to nabbing the culprits.

First Case of Beers was published by Forty Press in 2014. It is available from Amazon and BarnesAndNoble.com.

Bet on Beers follows the crew to Las Vegas, where priceless artifacts, including a jade bathtub, have gone missing at the casino store owned by Johnny Scalabrino. Once again, Beers and company are called on to find the perpetrators while navigating the dangerous, high-stakes world of gambling.

This time, murder is on the agenda, and Beers suspects he is out of his league. The heists seem impossible, particularly the theft of the bathtub. A parallel assault on the casino's gambling operation complicates the investigation. Once again, a musical solution presents itself and Beers is able to answer the riddle of this baffling case.

Bet on Beers was published by Forty Press in 2016. It is available from Amazon and BarnesAndNoble.com.

When the head of a sportswriter, a former co-worker at the Minnesota Herald, appears in the store, Beers discovers a long list of suspects. Everyone wanted Harry Devin dead, or so it seems.

Beers Ahead follows the brain trust through a macabre investigation that lends an even creepier vibe to the Halloween season. Complications distract Beers from his task—mainly oversight of a construction project and a new honey to woo.

A mysterious stranger, a secret correspondent, a vintage chapeau and an unpublished manuscript are some of the elements the team encounters as the complex scheme unfolds. But Beers always has music to guide him down the right path.

Beers Ahead was released by Liquid Rabbit Publishing in 2018. It is available from Amazon and BarnesAndNoble.com.

Follow PM LaRose on Facebook. More information on Jim Biersovich can be discovered at the Beers Detective Agency on Facebook.

Made in the USA
Coppell, TX
13 February 2020

15684303R00125